THE
THIRST
FOR
BLOOD

Other books written by Ashaki Boelter:

Doomed School
Beware of a Cat's Fury
The Nok
Witch Momma, Dummy for Hire
Destined To Win
The Bloody Curse of Humankind

The Thirst for Blood

A Novel

Ashaki Boelter

Shakalot High Entertainment

The Thirst for Blood

Ashaki Boelter
Sacramento, California

Library of Congress

Cataloging-in-Publication Data

ISBN: 978-0-9796219-7-0

All illustrations © by Ashaki Boelter
Cover by
Printed in the USA by
Lulu Enterprise
3131 RDU Center, Suite 210
Morrisville, NC 27560

Published by Shakalot High Entertainment
Edited In-House Shakalot High
Shakalot High Entertainment books may be ordered through various online booksellers

Dedicated to my close friends and family

Table of Contents

"They will be punished with eternal destruction, forever separated from the Lord and his glorious power." (New Living Translation Bible, 2nd Thessalonians 1: 9)

NOT suitable for children due to references to drugs, language, sex, and adult themes.

Chapter 1
The Host

Throughout suffocated crevices and shadowy hillsides, the martyr of night celebrated a cast of darkness atop an unmarked, speedy 1980 Caprice. Inside of the fatally-aged, sewn, and impending blackened casket on four deflated wheels, a self-made raider, and notorious thief cautiously and periodically glanced into his rearview mirror. Without caution to the wind and reckless abandonment to any speculative ambush of the law, his greed of money and hunger for power drove him into the secluded, sleeping valley of San De Juan.

One enormous gulp of strong liquor, unbeknownst to his final, the criminal aimlessly threw the empty wine bottle out the window and parked in an alley behind the city bank. After placing his black ski cap over his head, he crept to the backdoor of the bank in adjuration, found simplicity in disarming the alarm, and disengaging an outdated lock.

He greedily rubbed his hands in gratification to his luck, for he had no indebtedness to any godly faith even as the respective moonlight pierced the darkness like a pin upon the keyhole. He simply chuckled and praised his practiced prowess upon cracking open the bank safe to the tune of half a million.

"Hey! You had better drop that bag of money and put your hands up right now!"

Two short security officers held the thief at gunpoint, while the hideously outdated alarm bell unpunctually sounded! The surrendered thief pondered a combative escape, as the security officers cautiously approached.

"Keep your fucking hands ups!" A security officer violently pulled the slide back on his gun. "Make one move, and I swear that I will blow your brains out. Do you understand?"

The other security officer kicked the thief's money bag away and then began to frisk while he mischievously stared at his coworker, who, in turn, now stared at the bag of money. Finished with patting the thief down to the toes for any other weapons, the security officer backed away, without noting the small gun hidden underneath and in the back of the thief's mask.

With his gun cocked and loaded, the security officer that blocked the front entrance turned off the alarm by punching numbers on a keypad. He then locked the front door and radioed into the police department over the talkie on his shoulder. "Barney Hines, this is Hot Rod 2 over. Go on and have the police cancel a 10-90 for the bank. I repeat, you cancel that 10-90."

"Copy that, Hot Rod 2. What happened down there?"

The security officer answered, "Faulty wires caused the bank alarm; we did not find any sign of forced entry. So, there's no crime committed here; the situation is clear. We'll take a look at the cameras anyhow, but we're all clear here. Roger, Hot Rod 2 out."

"It takes one criminal to know another," whispered the smiley thief.

"Sir, you get out of here before I change my mind and call the police back here," demanded the security officer, as he waved his gun.

"Is that so?"

"We never saw your face or took your wallet to check you out. So, I want you to turn around, head out that back door, return to that hunk-of-junk car of yours in the alley, drive off and crawl back under the rock in from which you came. Do you understand, boy?"

"Yeah," added the other security officer, surely not the sharpest knife in the drawer. "We never had you remove your mask to see your face, and we disengaged the camera. So, go on and split."

"I suppose you guys expect me to leave without my money?"

"So, he has jokes now," chuckled the dopey security officer. "He's stuck on stupid."

"Guys, we all know that as soon as I walk out that back door and drive away, you two underpaid flashlight cops will take this bag of money for yourself and write up some claim that there was surely a theft, but the thief got away."

"What? Sir, you've blindly mistaken our hospitality in this!"

"Oh? How have I done that?"

"Well, first of all," added the other security officer with the waving gun still pointed at the thief, "the reason we're letting you get away is that we can see that you're obviously down on your luck by just the way you are dressed like some kind of strung-out meth addict and smell like booze. I am giving you a chance on life by letting you go, scot-free!"

"Chance on life? You goons want the money for yourselves!"

"Hey! My friend is a saint!" shouted the dopey security officer, who mockingly made the Sign of the Cross with his now gun in hand. "Praise the Lord because he is also a forgiving man for letting you go. And if we did keep any of the money, you'd better believe that this saint would give it away for tithes and offerings this Sunday! Well, at least he'd give ten percent."

The other security officer declared, "I believe in God. I go to church. I'm a shoo-in for heaven."

"Alright…! I've heard enough!" The thief stared a hole through the security officers. "I do not believe in a God, but if there was one, you two are certainly mocking whatever the hell a Father or Jesus Christ said in a stinking Bible. You're both as thieving and conniving as I, a bunch of sinners and low life hypocrites. So, where does that leave you two dumb fucks going in your twisted beliefs?"

"Sir, I believe you're telling my friend and me that we are going to hell?"

"Well," replied the thief, who quickly grabbed his miniature gat from underneath the back of his mask, "I certainly wouldn't go to this light!"

Suddenly, bright flashes flared from bank windows, whereas only candescent throughout the darkness of a sleeping town from the Sheriff's office window, atop the highest surround hill. And within the loud pops of his defeated and decayed gum, peculiar and off-rhythm cracks permeated his nonchalant chews within his hearing senses. Without hesitation, he ordered the graveyard shift police to immediately infect the streets of the small town like a terrible plague of possessed fireflies; all lights and somewhat inexperienced, bookworm graduates with little to no experience toward any dangerously criminal misconduct to this nature.

As he drank to the victory of robbing a bank and lighting up two flashlight cops, the thief now owned half a million dollars in his trunk. The thief drove over one hundred miles per hour and realized that his vehicle was spotted by a police helicopter above. Several of the town's most excellent police in cars quickly closed in too.

The thief blazed across the empty dark road and nearly ten miles away from the small town he robbed, the hopeful-half-millionaire saw that the stretch ahead was wide open. There weren't any turnoffs to any homes or even cities to shake cops. The only option he had for escape was to turn off the main road and challenge their newer, tax-rewarded flimsy produced vehicles to an off-terrain, rocky pursuit. With his weighty steel car, he jumped off the road and roasted towards the hills and plentiful forests.

Within minutes, as he anticipated, the entire police fleet peeled off the road after him. The chopper remained above him. He looked right and left ahead, as the glorious moonlight gave him guidance in all direction. To his avail, there were no openings between the hills to drive his car over or through. The only hope he noticed was a hole with boards and rocks blocking the entrance.

"Sir," the pilot of the chopper radioed the sheriff, "the driver is headed for Skull Mine. Sheriff, should we try to gun him down? I do not believe he is going to stop at this point."

Back at the precinct, Sheriff Edward Sherman closed his office door. He leaned over his radio mic and answered, "You listen here. We've been around here for a long time and know what's in that mine. Nobody or nothing is to disturb that mine! You had better do whatever you have to do to stop that lunatic from getting in there. Do you hear me?"

"Copy that, sheriff!"

At closer speculation, the thief realized that he needed to decide his direction quickly. He pulled his gun and aimed out his window to buy time to slow down and think. Still, his decisional resolution came sooner because the chopper above shot a round of bullets at his car, and one of the scattered shots nearly blew his shoulder entirely off!

There went his cartwheeling gun into the stampede of police cars behind.

"Son of a bitch, you shot me in the arm!" The thief's usually rounded shoulder now opened like a blossomed red rose, while his clavicle bone broke upwards and sat against his ear. Blood and body fat splattered across his face in the wind and slid across his noggin like a black widow's thick web into his back seat. He was not able to take another shot like that!

The pursued car speedily approached the heavily boarded-up mine. The thief figured there were only a few outcomes: He could pull over and surrender, drive through the heavy boards and search for an escape route inside the mine or simply crash and explode into the side of the hill at the entrance.

"Give me liberty with half-a-million dollars or give me death!"

The thief hammered his old school car into the hillside barricade, as a horizontal mushroom cloud of fire and dust exploded out into the police stampede! All of the police cars stopped at the entrance. Everybody could see that the vehicle drove a distance inside the cave before disappearing into the blackness.

"The fugitive entered the cave," said the police officer in the chopper. "He cannot be seen. I don't think he will live very long, as I nearly shot off his arm. Do you know if there is another entrance, sheriff? Do you want us to continue pursuit into the cave?"

The sheriff shook his head and pounded his hand on his desk. "I know that the cave has no outlet. I used to navigate it when I was a young lad. The getaway car wasn't registered. I see no good in filling our jail space up with any more filth tonight. The driver took the lives of two neighbors of mines at the bank tonight. He's made his bed; he'll have to lie in it. I want the entrance destroyed! We'll simply dig him out and get the money out of there later this week when he's all but dead. Bury that son of a bitch! Do you hear me? Bury him!"

"So, how do we write this up in a report if we're not in pursuit of the arrest?"

"I'll take care of any damn report," answered the sheriff. "One thing that I know is that we're not going to let this situation ruin next weekend's hosting of our very first and nationally televised wrestling event! Do you know how much revenue is coming into our town from sponsors and fans from all over the United States who love wrestlers like Lumberjack Jones, Crane, and Gravity Warrior? With the revenue we're going to rake in for our city, we're going to build this place into a metro, like a San Francisco or a New York City! Maybe we can even build a large amusement park and host a bunch of ducks or mice in costumes like out there in California! I'm not going to let this little thief steal our thunder!"

"Uh… Who is Lumberjack Jones or Crane?"

"You're not a pro wrestling fan, eh? How do you live with yourself?"

Chapter 2

Arisen

One single light at the end of the tunnel, a faint flame that signaled the beginning of a new life as it were at the beginning of time, one man birthed from unconsciousness in swelling pain sat alone in his silent car holding a lighter. And when he saw no cops, it was good.

The half-a-millionaire miraculously awakened from passing out after he crashed in the tunnel, for a chance at a compromised survival, partially learning of his grim fate to come. Behind his car was pure gloom! The entrance to the cave tightly piled with many feet of stone. The police had buried him alive.

"There's no way those stones are permanent," chuckled the thief. He dug out a box of cigarettes from his pants pocket with two bloody fingers, nearly burnt himself with the lighter, pulled out a stick, lit it, and plugged it between his lips. He lit it. "I'm sure they'll try to wait for me to die in here before they come for the money. I got to find a way out of here, but first, I got to see what I got to survive."

He took a mental inventory of his food and drinks. Within his car, he found: Half of a molded granola bar under the driver seat, a bag of expired peanuts in the glove compartment, and a couple of beers in the trunk. Without reluctance, he drank a beer to keep his mind off the pain that came from his shredded and bloody shoulder. Now he had one beer.

Already that kind of bloody pain expended a lot of his energy that he could not spare, so he had to do more about it. With his one arm, as he held the lighter, he pushed his protruded clavicle back into his left shoulder and under the skin so that it did not poke his ear anymore. He used his ski mask to slow the bleeding and as a bandage on his shoulder. Then he held the lighter towards the walls of the cave.

"There has got to be a way out of here."

Suddenly, he noticed the lighter flame lean towards a crack in the wall and smoke entered. It appeared to be a wall made by men with plenty of rocks. What was on the other side of those rocks and boards? Perhaps there were tools, weapons, or even food beyond. With little to no other option served for his curiosity, the thief pulled rocks from the wall.

Once he was able to climb inside, he held up his lighter and saw bats hanging at the far wall and in the middle of the space, a bunch of wooden boxes marked Do Not Open. The first thought he had was that everything belonged to the military or government. Never in his entire life would he have believed in what he was to find.

"Why would anyone build this room, just to leave an urn full of ashes in a box?" That is what he found in the first box he opened. "Religious people don't make any sense to me. Just put the ashes back in the dirt and call it a day! What else is in here?"

So, he busted open the other boxes and crates to find invaluable maps and official papers to his utter agitation. However, the last box he opened had a considerable amount of various and expired wine from the early 1800s! He figured that either he was stuck in the cave forever to drink himself into time-traveling or death or he was going to bust out of the cave soon enough with a half a million dollars and now the most expensive and sellable wine. The box of old wine had to find a way into his trunk. He quickly loaded that wooden box onto his right shoulder and headed for his car.

"Whoa!" He stumbled over a rock! To avoid a disaster of any broken glasses of wine and a broken heart, he maneuvered to stabilize the box on his shoulder. The ski mask he used for a bandage fell towards the ground. He aggressively tried to catch it in mid-air, but he spun and inadvertently knocked over the nearby urn with his buttocks. Ashes flew in every direction!

The lonely thief was covered in ash, while his bloody and meaty shoulder was notably exposed. He grabbed his ashy ski hat and then walked over and placed the wooden box of alcohol in his trunk next to the bag of money.

Ash that sat upon his shoulder began to smoke, bubble up, and liquefy into a blackened web that seemed to come alive and connect with other veins on his body. Suddenly, his clavicle bone cracked a few times, but only as he witnessed miraculous healing!

The thief began to suffocate and spit out black smoke, while blackened blood ran from his mouth. His vision became impaired by his blood; he now knew then that the ashes had poisoned his entire being. There was excruciating pain throughout his whole upper body, as he dropped to one knee and loosely held himself up by the back bumper. More and more bats flew from the hole in the tunnel and came to feast upon his flesh. He could not fight them off with one skinned hand and a lighter any longer.

"If I can't have this money, nobody can have it!" declared the thief. Left with his passion of greed, his strongest trait, he tossed the lit lighter into the car's gas tank, located behind the license plate. There was suddenly darkness in the tunnel.

The elevated sounds of frenzied bats that fed on the struggling and tortured thief that begged for an explosion was terror!. Along with the ripping and shredding of his body he could hear, he felt every single stapling bite and tear from his face, his stomach, his biceps, his pelvis, his groin, his thighs, to his feet; bats pulled and popped away pieces of his flesh in clumps. After the pain stopped, he slipped into inexistence with fear of his relentless non-belief in an afterlife.

With one humanly last fight for life, the surrendered newborn agnostic and fearless thief angrily cried to the heavens in his last gasp,

"Damn you! You did this to me! I hate you!" And his throat was then brutally picked apart like outdated pomegranates or wilted red cabbage, ground and savagely devoured by violent bats in a rain of red and an outpouring of drool.

Within seconds, the car exploded in one single light and ripped apart any living creature in that tunnel; that was not good for all humanity. To be free of death and from the hard bondage of the so-called tomb of Skull Mine, the last words of the shredded thief came to favor of a once defeated and caged monster that walked the earth, a soulless mystery of the world's darkest truth. Cruelly rejected from the desired perishing of hell, to suffer eternity as an unwanted plague to humans, his very existence stirred the madness of living man to hunt for his extinction.

The starved beast only thirsted for human blood, as the water of the womb referred to family, which he had none. Those that defied his need for a deathly bond would get robbed of blood, life, and judgment. That private misfortune was the opposition to how the universe moved and taught by the Creator's word. That contretemps warranted the destruction of hell, but only if broken by something of hell.

Sir Sange, a soulless, rogue beast of neither heaven nor hell, a virus or plague manifested into a man, threatened the existence of all dimensions of the earth. He frequently died, but mistakenly had been awakened by man's incompetence so often. Was there a sentence to those who'd errored in their fault? Should he bite you, the punished undead shared in his exclusion of heaven or hell, or life, as long as he walked the earth.

After the fire exhausted in Skull Hill, what remained of the mysterious ashes within the crushed urn and the bloody guts of the thief, was a resurrected villain.

THE THIRST FOR BLOOD

The cursed male stared down the dark tunnel at the light that shined at the entrance. Punished from being seen by the heavens and the Creator's fire of the sun or likeness in death wherein humankind's eruditeness of holy weapons, his abomination to earth was left to parry his repeatedly desired existence in the moonlit darkness.

He anxiously waited for sundown to exit and quench his thirst for blood. With his reddened eyes fixed upon the end of the dimming tunnel, the resurrected beast could smell the blood of the close population.

Chapter 3

Blind Lies

That early fall, the withered tree leaves sifted through softer, calm winds, while the late morning was brightest in San De Juan to those who were not keen on the murders committed at the bank last night. At the current hour of the morning, the police investigation and newscasters reporting came to an end. An old police chopper finished monitoring the area for any further circumstances and returned to the police precinct on the hill. The last couple of police officers removed the yellow tape that was wrapped around the bank, as nearby businesses opened.

"We'll leave after we finish these delicious donuts," stated Officer Theodore Bowie. He and his partner, Officer Michelle Achebe, watched a bunch of teenagers head into Levi's Coffee Stop. It was a popular hangout for delicious and affordable food. "Michelle, I know for a fact that one or two of those young punks have a suspended license because I'm the one who gave them a ticket recently! I guess they can't resist the girls in there; they'd rather break the law for a little booty. That's a damn shame!"

"Lighten up, Theo. After all, you were once a young horny teen at some point too. And you're one to talk. You're married, player."

"I'm a player? Me? No, I am just a stone-cold and separated gentleman."

"Oh?" Officer Achebe fluttered her lashes. "Yes, you are separated, but you're still married! You're a player because I still have a pair of your draws in my dresser and teeth marks on my ass, while your wife at home is waiting for you to get your act together, get counseling, and move out of that hotel."

"I ain't going back to that woman. There isn't anything left to Jill and me except divorce costs. I'm good to go! I showed you that the other night at the hotel."

"You sure did, player." Officer Achebe massaged her partner's upper thigh.

Suddenly a loud sports car roared up the street and aggressively parked in the lot of Levi's Coffee Stop. As the boyfriend and girlfriend cops, under incognito, surveyed from across the street, four familiar and well documented young men from the high school football team jumped out of the sports car and sprinted into the restaurant.

Levi's Coffee Stop was also a teenager's hang out, as it served not only great food, but it had arcade games, a refurbished jukebox with hip hop, and plenty of enormous television screens for sports events. During the nights, the bar and dance floor operated until the early morning.

"So, nobody heard about a bank break-in late last night?" One of the young men that just started a job at Levi's conversed with his classmates at their favorite table near the front of the restaurant. "I closed up last night. I know something happened across the street!"

"I haven't heard anything," answered one of his friends.

"On my way out the door, I heard the bank alarm briefly go off!" The employee ducked when his manager walked by. "I figured it must have been a false alarm because I did see security officers in the bank. They seemed to be talking, the way he spoke with his hands. Rideshare came to pick me up right then, but I swear that I heard gunshots when we were about a block away. Then a whole bunch of squad cars passed by us! It was around two. This morning, they pulled away from the yellow tape."

"Dude, here comes your manager."

"Get back to work!" shouted Levi, the owner of the restaurant. "Get back here and bust those suds, boy! I don't pay you for lollygagging with your friends!"

"I swear I'm going to quit this new job," said the angry teen. "The boss here, Levi, sucks. Besides, I am starting to think that this part of the town isn't safe at night! Somebody has to know something about what I heard last night. I heard gunshots; I'm sure of that!"

"Nope," replied another teen. "I haven't read about or seen anything like that on the news this morning about a bank robbery. Trust me when I say that I would know because my grandpa gets up at 4 am to watch all the news. He told me he was up a little earlier due to a small earthquake, but otherwise, he would have said something."

"Maybe your grandpa was doing something else that early, acting like he felt an earthquake," laughed the hottest senior in the high school named Jenny. "Isn't that the same hour that the yoga lady with the stripe down her tights, comes on television and bends her ass all over for the world to see?"

"Screw you, Jen!" He threw his new apron on the floor and walked off the job.

Jenny was the Obama High School blunder in looks and personality compared only to her magnificent mother, who was the Miss Obama High Princess of the school in 1978. Other than that, Jenny was the hottest and most flexible cheerleader, the boldest athlete in how she wore her threads a couple sizes too small and looked fantastic with winning or losing, and the most desired female attraction of the senior class today!

Every young man in the school district wanted a chance to at least touch a fingertip on her body, but there was only one young man she was interested in and whom she deemed appropriate to bring home for her law enforcement mother to meet. Yet, there she stood across from a chunky jock with a buzz cut that believed his ex-waiter pal. Maybe there was truth to a bank robbery across the street last night?

"You are lucky you're somewhat hot, Jenny. Nobody talks about my friend's grandpa and gets away with it except you." With a glance at her bulging cleavage, Jessup licked his lips. He grimaced when his rocky tongue hit a crusty cold sore on his mouth. "You made the poor guy quit his job. Damn. So, did you hear anything? We all know that your mom is a cop."

Alongside Jessup, was his childhood friend, Demarcus Peeler. He just walked up. For a second, he caught Jenny's eyes, for she looked right through Jessup. She was so into Demarcus that he had to responsibly shake her off before she near climaxed in her seat! However, he looked past her at the bank across the street.

"There's a cop car sitting in the alley next to the bank."

"Demarcus," said Jenny, "maybe they're just keeping an eye on the future Francisco County inmate standing next to you."

Jessup replied, "Very funny. When you graduate from high school, you should join a circus with jokes like those, but any cage they put you in, you'd look like a stripper."

"Well, any cage you're in, we'd all feed you a bunch of bananas!" Jenny laughed.

"Whatever." Jessup looked across the street also. "My homeboy is right. There is a cop car sitting over there. Something had to have gone down last night."

"Why doesn't somebody just go out and ask those police?"

As he cooked over the hot stove, Levi shouted and cursed from the smoky kitchen. "Stop talking to your friends and come get these orders to the tables! The plates are stacking up with food! Where's that lazy boy I hired? Where is everybody going? Hey, come back!"

As gathered teens from the restaurant approached the nearly hidden police car, Officer Achebe snapped out of her euphoria and quickly removed her partner's caressing fingers from under her skin-clad uniform. "Oh no, Theodore, not right now! Theo! The kids from the restaurant are coming this way! Oh shit. That's my daughter too! I can't hide anything from her. Let's get out of here! Start the car! Start the damn car!"

"What? Are you serious?" Officer Bowie inappropriately glanced at her daughter, Jenny. "That's your daughter? Whoa! She has grown up a bit since I've last seen her!"

"Turn on the siren," ordered his partner, who adjusted her clothing and sat up. "Turn on the lights; we have to split. Come on! Please! Go! Go!"

Officer Achebe's partner disappointedly did everything she asked of him and skidded away down the street before the teens could get there to ask anything about what occurred in the wee morning.

Even if those cops had known, it was only a partial truth. Therefore, it would have been a lie. The rest of what happened earlier today was soon to be discovered, as the old police chopper cautiously surveyed Skull Hill.

"Sheriff," the pilot radioed to the police station. "Sheriff Sherman, I need to talk to you. We need to talk on this private channel. Sheriff Sherman, do you read me? Pick up."

"This is Sheriff Edward Sherman. I read you. What is so important that you need that much privacy? Copy."

"It is about Skull Hill, sir."

After immediately switching to a private frequency, both men anticipated the discussion.

"Sheriff, the rock barrier at the entrance has been removed."

"That is strange, said the sheriff. He turned off his mini television.

"We blasted those rocks at the entrance earlier, and there had to be at least twenty feet of blockage into that hill. There is no way somebody could remove the rocks unless they blasted it with a missile, or there was a lot of dynamite inside."

"Do we have a visual of what's inside the cave? Maybe the thief's car exploded?"

"To hell if I'm going inside that cave to find out, sheriff!"

"You got a gun, don't you?" asked the sheriff. "Have some nuts about it and get down there, Officer Brown."

"Have you forgotten about what is buried in that cave?"

"Damn it, Joshua!" screamed the sheriff. "Of course, I have not forgotten. It's a tomb with a box of some loony magician's ashes buried deep in the walls of the cave."

"Please tell me that you did not just call that thing a loony magician?"

"After all these years," replied the sheriff, "I still have haunting memories of what that guy pulled and had us believing. Last night, I cannot believe that I acted scared out of a distorted teenage experience. We should've entered Skull Hill and arrested the thief that shot down two of our town's security guards and robbed our bank."

"What's in that cave is a real creature, sir!"

"Come on, Joshua. You know that while we served in Romania, over half of our brigade was on mushrooms; we would've believed that the magician was an alien if they told us that."

"Let me remind you," said Officer Brown. "You and I, along with the rest of our U.S. troops, helped take down that devil in Romania. Do you not remember? The bloody bastard took out several of our military's best from its castle! There wasn't a bullet or grenade that could stop him! We all watched it kill our friends Sam Barley, Kemp, and Sargent Topper. It sucked them dry of their blood!"

"Sam… Yeah, I remember him."

"Then you remember that it took a noble, young traveler by the name of Van Helsing, who had inherited family knowledge of how to defeat such a beast, to help us counter that ungodly monster," reminded Officer Brown.

The sheriff irresistibly recalled. "Yes."

"It was Van Helsing that said, and I clearly remember that this immortal monster always found ways to come back time and time again. He also told me in private that he believed the vampire used telepathy to summon faithless humans into bad judgment to resurrect it."

"That Van Helsing surely had a way with stories." The sheriff pondered. "You have to wonder if partial ashes of a vampire could form into the full figure of that creature."

"Anything is possible with that terror, Edward. I would say yes!"

The sheriff shook his head with candid boredom. "Look, my friend. If a vampire arose from partial ashes, conventional wisdom says that he'd have a partial body. He'd wake up to find he's missing a leg, an arm, or even his fangs! Can you imagine a vampire trying to kill from a wheelchair or attacking with a white cane?"

"Sheriff, are you on medication? I do not think anything is funny."

"Come on, Josh! I think the Romanian government and Van Helsing knew what they were doing when they spread the man's ashes up and put the urns on different continents. They were trying to kick us out from occupying their land; we were not the most honorable troops at the time."

"We were a lively group."

Sheriff Sherman pointed to the roof and declared, "I would've made up a vampire story to get rid of us too. We drank like maniacs out there and played lots of games with the gypsies. They wanted us gone! The man in the castle was a lunatic, and they wanted him gone."

Officer Brown felt comforted. "Perhaps you're right, sheriff. I'm just at awe with how the driver I shot, while in pursuit, drove directly into the mine. You're saying it was simply chance. Here I thought that maybe vampire ashes had some kind of brain telepathy to direct people."

"Are you listening to yourself?"

"Yeah, you're right. Vampires cannot exist. Maybe I need medication."

"They have a lot of history with witchcraft in Romania," explained the sheriff. "We were young and did all kinds of drugs and mushrooms on our tour out there. There is no telling what kind of hallucinations we were exposed to while we occupied that land."

"We were pretty out of it then, weren't we?"

"The monster you thought we fought at that castle in Romania," continued the sheriff, "was a local magician that was ahead of his time and played with our nightmares we created from Hollywood movies. He used smoke tablets and expensive mechanical props to fake everybody out. Some of the props he used helped stage the death of troops that, but in reality, they ran from the military."

"You're saying that none of our fellow troops got killed out there? It was an act?"

"None of ours died. The whole vampire show was a smokescreen for those who ran from the military, while the rest of us were high on drugs. Nobody knew what was going on."

"I'll be damned. How did you find out about this?"

"A few years back, I did my Internet search of every one of those men in our camp that we thought the magician killed," stated the sheriff. "I got curious after I came across a mysterious email from one of the troops named Topper."

"I remember Topper!"

"He was probably senile and losing his heath to his ailing infliction when he hit the Send-All button in an email to his doctor. Our friend Sam Barley now lives in Alabama and is a plumber, Kemp passed away five years ago of natural causes, and Topper who goes by Richard Martin is living out his life in an Oregon convalescent home. You and I got duped about some monster's ashes that we buried in Skull Hill."

"How long ago did you learned about all this?"

"About ten years ago."

"Now wait for just a second, sheriff," said Officer Brown. "I saw the ashes in the urn; I was there to see it buried at Skull Hill."

"Our last night there in Romania," explained the sheriff, "I received the ashes. As it turns out, he accumulated a lot of gambling debt from important foreign leaders, so he was executed right underneath our noses. They covered it up by spreading his ashes. As with the other officials from world governments, our hands were not clean due to some of our dirtiest officials when it came to gambling with the magician. So, in the end, we all got his ashes to satisfy the debt. Outside of that, I cannot divulge any more top secret information regarding who ordered this or that."

"So the urn with ashes has been a top-secret thing all these years."

"Only some of our regime found out about it."

"And you continued to allow me to think there was a real vampire in that cave, which cause all kinds of stress-related medical issues in my recent years?"

"I swore to protect the information and you from being involved." The sheriff lit a cigarette in his chair. "Joshua, I'll have some men get out there and then demolish the mine once and for all. You can call it a day."

Officer Brown turned the chopper back towards the city. "I can't believe that you had me believing in monsters for all these years. I have been worried sick since I retired from the military! Not to mention, I have had a ton of vampire nightmares!"

"I hope that you're still open to believing in professional wrestling. You did not forget that I got tickets from the mayor for this weekend's event for our officers, right? I'll be gone for the day to go and pick them up. The mayor and I will be playing a little golf today. Just come back by here tonight, and I'll hand you a ticket."

"Well, you old bastard sheriff, you've still got me believing that pro wrestling is real. Hold onto my tickets! I'll come by your office before I retire for the night. I am over and out!"

Officer Joshua Brown surveyed the city from the police chopper. Still, he remained profoundly confused at how calm the sheriff seemed that afternoon than in the earlier morning hour when he frantically directed for the cave to be immediately sealed off after the thief entered.

By Ashaki Boelter

Chapter 4

Inherited Duplicity

Sunlight succumbed into puked layers of dreadfully yellow flu phlegm and bloodied snot, into the horizon, as the risen night moon reined victory over the sky like a shiny sword poking Skull Hill. An American construction company and a cast of nervous police officers explored the dark tunnel of Skull Hill under the instruction of Sheriff Edward Sherman for recovery of half-a-million dollars stolen from the city bank and the responsible thief.

Outside of the old mine, tractors began to move enormous stones and boulders towards the entrance, guided by plenty of LED work lights. Inside the mine, a crew of miners and some police officers walked through the decade-old tunnel, fifty yards in length. They inspected the hidden room that once treasured boxes of wine and the mysterious box on the ground next to an empty, broken urn. Upon searching the car, nothing more than an extinguished piece of framing, there was no sign of any money or a body. There was a bunch of busted bottles in the trunk.

"The guy blew himself up," said Officer Bowie to Detective Bradbury. "Case closed."

Detective Bradbury was a heavyset man who was a professional from an esteemed college outside of the country. He had served many successful years in law enforcement, but even he seemed intrigued. He took notes and measured the effects of the explosion."

"Can we get out of here now? This place gives me the creeps." Officer Bowie cringed. He wanted to hold the hand of Officer Achebe, who stood nearby and studied the very same mystery alongside another officer. "There was no way the guy escaped."

"Well," said Detective Vincent Bradbury, who surveyed the floors and walls with his flashlight, "if the guy indeed blew himself up, where are his shattered bones or fragments of his flesh? All we found is a measly lighter. Nobody sees any other way out of here. We've gone over every inch of this cave. However, to my recollection, I have seen a mystery like so, but I'm afraid that the case eludes my forgiving conscience to speak on it. The internal misery, the pain he is imprisoned by, he has wielded that ax before with death."

Officer Bowie didn't catch half of what the detective rattled off in a distinct accent. "Perhaps with the gasoline in the car, money, and the volume of wine he found, the thief blew himself up to smithereens?"

From his knees, Detective Bradbury looked up and chuckled at Officer Bowie. "You're not the sharpest knife in the drawer when it comes to investigations. Help me up."

"I just report it how I see it." Officer Bowie paid little attention as to how he helped the detective up, as he noted from a distance that his interest was working a little too closely with the officer. There was a little bit of giggling between Officer Achebe and the obvious rookie.

"And how are we doing over here?" asked Officer Bowie. He held his chest high and even placed his enormous sunglasses on in the darkened cave. "What are we laughing at?"

"Oh," giggled Officer Achebe, "Officer Prendergast and I got a kick out of discussing a recent situation on the most recent wrestling show. They're going to pick up the storyline here this weekend in town. He's a big fan of the show, and he's got first row tickets!"

Officer Prendergast extended his hand to Officer Bowie. "I'm sorry, Officer Bowie? I'm Officer Cecil Prendergast of Sting County. The mayor instructed me to come here to help you all out in investigating possibly a mutual thief since we are right on the county line. Our local supermarket got held up about two days ago; we think this is the same guy that wiped them clean and shot up two customers. He's certainly a wanted man."

Officer Bowie did not extend his hand. "Well, we know that already. And what gives with everybody from the detective and now you, having strong accents? I don't understand half of anything anybody is saying in here."

"Okay… Well, I dig the accent." Officer Achebe bit her lip. She saw what was going on with her boy-toy, cop partner; she ignored further flirtation of the other officer. "So… Officer Bowie, did the detective find anything. Can we leave now? It is getting seriously late and past my shift. It looks as if the construction crew left us just enough space to walk out of here too, so the air is getting a little thin around here."

"If I can make out any of what the detective said, he's closing up the investigation, I think," replied Officer Bowie. However, he would not take his eyes off of Officer Prendergast, a near-flawless male that was tall and debonair, yet sinisterly pale with the voice of tuba chords. He could tell that the ominous officer was head over hills for Officer Achebe because he stared at her for way too long, in his opinion.

Officer Achebe looked at Officer Prendergast and wished he wasn't so brave. "Thank you for your help, Officer Prendergast. It was nice to have met you. Good luck with your investigation."

However, Officer Prendergast would not remove his eyes from Officer Michelle Achebe. In that split second, he was mesmerized by her natural biracial beauty of somebody he once passionately loved, a sensational sight of medieval art of a woman, past or present. Officer Prendergast roughly stripped her clean of her beige clad uniform in his daydream. He used his oily hand to descend her veiny neck to her juicy, soft melons. A warmer sensation, he cupped one and gently fingered her rocky orbit around her elongated, dark nipple.

He leaned into her aroma of Lavandula angustifolia and sweet coconut, placed his tongue on her sweaty abdomen and licked up and then down, between every sugary crevice and through black, wildly forestry and a fossilized dam of an abundant river of life. His eyes sat fixed on a single prize; his eyes storied the pinnacle of her gravest indulgence of deathful sex.

The magnificent officer dreamt of making dynamite love to her so profoundly passionate that it was Officer Achebe that snapped out of his hypnotic fantasy! Was it possible that time stood still for one second, as she experienced an overbearing climax in his eyes alone?

"Oh my," whispered Officer Achebe.

"Hey buddy," interrupted Officer Bowie, "I believe that she already said thank you for your help! Why don't you go over there and find more fingerprints or something."

"And I certainly appreciated it." Officer Prendergast winked at her. "You... are welcomed."

"Well," said Officer Achebe, in the middle of two men, "Officer Bowie and I should be on our way now. Come on, Officer Bowie. It's time to go."

"Listen, pal," mentioned Officer Bowie to Officer Prendergast, "I know that we do not have a problem here. She is off-limits. Do I make myself clear?"

"Forgive me, sir. I was not aware that her father was a police officer. Allow me to extend my deepest apologies. I meant no disrespect." Officer Prendergast nodded to both.

Officer Bowie was livid! "I am not her father, but who I am to her is none of your fucking business! Like I said, and I won't repeat it, she is off-limits. Do I make myself clear?"

"I'm nobody's property," added Officer Achebe. "I do not see any rings on these fingers. Now, cut the macho shit. Let's go. I haven't seen my daughter all day."

Officer Bowie angrily glanced at Officer Prendergast and joined Officer Achebe to leave the mine. Detective Bradbury accompanied the two from the tunnel, but when he passed Officer Prendergast, he stopped.

Detective Bradbury had a distant feeling, a slight recollection of Officer Prendergast's presence; he turned around and watched him depart into the hidden room to help others close up the investigation.

The detective was inclined to retire the case for tonight, yet his sagacity and awakened instincts alarmed him of unforeseen danger. Yet, he shook it off until he had a moment to extract his thoughts and learnings that perhaps were miscued by deceptions or truth. For now, there was a commotion outside of the cave between two women. That thwarted him further from the truth.

"Mom, what is going on out here?"

"Jenny!" Officer Achebe was surprised to see her daughter with some high school friends there. "What are you doing here? You need to go on back home."

"We have some questions about what happened last night at the bank," added Jessup.

Officer Bowie stood affront. "Just like Officer Achebe said, there is nothing to be seen here. We're only shutting down the mine. There is nothing to be seen."

Officer Achebe grabbed her daughter's arm and sternly said, "You know that you're not to follow me to any crime scene, young lady! You need to tell your friends that this is official police business and to get out of here. I'll be home a little late tonight."

Jenny blushed. "Wow, mom, now I see where I get a good taste in men. I have to say, the officer in the cave was much cuter than that rough partner of yours. That looked like a whole bunch of official police business going on in the cave, mother. By the way, what was his name? I believe it was Officer Cecil Prendergast."

"How do you know his name?"

Demarcus interrupted, "Your daughter just had to meet him."

"We spoke earlier," answered Jenny. "When we showed up, he had walked up and inquired about our business here. We told him that we worked in journalism for our school and that we wanted a story for the school paper! He said that we had to remain outside the cave, but we could look inside the tunnel to watch you, as long as we did not get in your way. He said it was fine, mom. He was super cute for an old guy, and his voice was so sexy!"

"Go home, Jenny! I am not going to ask you again."

"We're leaving," said Jenny, as she climbed into the back seat of Jessup's car. "I would date an older man if it was he! He has a great set of eyes and a nice ass! I think he wanted me!"

"He's out of your league, young lady!"

"Okay, mom," said Jenny, "but he is in yours!"

Jessup shook his head and spun his car around to head back to town. "Sorry Ms. Achebe, we'll get your daughter home!"

"You'd better!" Officer Achebe warned. "No funny games and drive like you got sense!"

Minutes later and after nightfall, the construction crew allowed the rest of the police officers and detectives to exit the mine. As instructed, the demolition team detonated Skull Hill and placed stones at the entrance.

Detective Bradbury called the sheriff on his cellular phone to let him know that they did not find much inside, from the money to the remains of the thief. The only educated guess was that the thief escaped somehow.

"Very well, then," replied Sheriff Sherman. "It's late. Why don't you return to the precinct? We'll go over what you found or any clues, Detective Bradbury."

"It's a Sunday night, and to be honest, it is the one night my wife and I have to unwind during the week. I'll need to take a raincheck for now. Plus, I need to research some possible clues and develop some photos. I have some time Wednesday if you are okay with that, sheriff. How does 10 AM sound? "

"Honestly, I prefer to work the late shifts, so how about 10 PM on Wednesday?"

"You're a persistent man tonight," replied the detective with a chuckle, "but I know those kinds of late hours will get the old lady to investigate me for moonlighting. Let me get back to you in the next few days; I'll see to it that we sit a spell at a decent hour. Right now, I'm going to walk on one's gums for the night."

"Oh?" Sheriff Sherman excitedly praised the detective. "Are you Dutch, detective? That was a Dutch expression, I believe."

"It runs in my family. You have a good ear, sheriff."

"No," replied the sheriff, "I am just familiar with the culture. You have yourself a great night, exhausted one. We will talk soon. Goodbye."

Honestly, everybody was tired at the current hour and, unfortunately, miles away and headed back to San De Juan. Officer Achebe certainly did not care for working the late-night, much less for Officer Bowie's behavior at the hill they just left. She claimed his response was not professional, uncalled for, disgusting, low, humiliating, unproductive, stupid, unwarranted, and unbecoming to her taste.

"Seriously, the guy looked at you like he wanted to hump your brains out! I wasn't having that, Michelle."

"I am yours for the taking," replied Officer Achebe, "and nobody else's! You do know that I'm going to get flirted with for the rest of my life. Am I right? You've got the hottest girl in town! Besides, I don't have any rings on these fingers. Until you divorce your wife, Jill, I won't sport any jewelry from you. So, you're going to have to deal with those to step up to this beautiful and hot woman."

"That's a low blow, Michelle! You didn't have to go there."

"And you know… There's one thing I need for you to understand, Theodore."

"What?"

"The one thing I don't want is a man that thinks I cannot handle my own damn business. I can handle guys like him; I don't need you to rescue me! I'm not some easy slut. So, you have nothing to worry about."

"I'm sorry."

"I have to admit that I am enjoying this jealous side of you, though. It's kind of cute."

"Yeah, well, you know, I had to let that sucker know what's up. I'm the man up in this bitch!"

Soon enough, Officer Bowie and Officer Achebe strolled to their respective locker rooms to change into their civilian clothing at the precinct. They passed the sheriff's door but did not talk to him because he signaled with his hand for them to keep moving.

Inside of the sheriff's office, Officer Joshua Brown sat in the chair in front of the oak desk. He watched his longtime pal Sheriff Edward Sherman slowly walked over to his bookshelf. He appeared to be thinking long and hard about something.

"Are you sure that you're feeling okay?" Officer Brown grimaced. "Edward, you're looking a little pale tonight. I think that you might want to take the night off. You may have caught wind of the flu or something like that."

"My old friend, I assure you that I have never, ever been better. I scorched the mayor on the golf course earlier and scored those wrestling event tickets. Here's one for you."

"Thanks, sheriff." Officer Brown received his pro wrestling ticket and slid it into his pocket.

"Excited?"

"Sure."

"So," said the sheriff, "it appears that none of the operations we sent to Skull Hill found any remains or the money, according to the report I read."

Officer Brown had not fully bought the sheriff's story. Even though it sounded humanly swell, it did not satisfy his memories of what he witnessed fifty years ago. All-day long, he still could not conjure up believing in what the sheriff told him about the façade of the magician in Romania. "I don't know sheriff. The story you told me seemed far-fetched."

"And believing in vampires doesn't? You seem to be in a mental dilemma, Officer Brown."

"I'm telling you, the thief got in there and disturbed a monster's sleep. I know what you told me earlier today, but my gut tells me that I am right. The story you told me is a cover-up!"

"Perhaps you should see a shrink, my friend."

"I'm sure of it," the officer stuttered. "Or maybe it's the other way around; the monster found him! It's the most logical sense to me that I can make of this mystery."

"You impress me with the vampire angle. So tell me this, Joshua. If they did not find the thief or his remains thereof, what exactly do you speculate happened?"

"The vampire ate him!"

"The vampire ate him?" The sheriff chuckled. "If so, I thought vampires only drank blood. I did not know they ate humans. Tell me, how did you become such a scholar of vampires?"

"You and I both saw with our own eyes, that real vampire! I don't know if he ate him or what, but I know it had something to do with his not being found in the cave. At least with an explosion, we would have found bones or blood-splatter."

Sheriff Sherman took another step closer to Officer Brown and bent over to tell him a secret. He whispered, "He knows who you are. He is watching you right now, Joshua."

Officer Brown jumped from the office chair! "What did you just say? Wait a minute…" He pulled his gun on the sheriff!

"I'm afraid that won't be necessary. Put your gun away, Joshua."

"He escaped and bit you, didn't he!"

The sheriff smiled and lowered his collar. There sat two deep teeth marks in the sheriff's neck. "You are a sagacious, old man Joshua."

"Where is he?" Officer Brown stumbled across the wall, headed for the door. "Where is the bloody monster? How did he get out?"

"If you want to ask him yourself, he'll be at the wrestling event this weekend at the town's high school football field. That is going to be a bloodbath extravaganza! The only setback you have is if you'll survive to make it there for all of the fun."

Officer Brown flipped around to the office door, opened it, and ran down the hallway with the undead sheriff in pursuit! Terrified, as the pale sheriff closed in, the pilot took to the stairwell and sprinted to the ceiling where his chopper sat.

He managed to get in the helicopter, lock the door, and start it. He flipped on the lights; the pale sheriff, with long fangs, stood right there in front of the chopper!

"Lord, Jesus!" screamed Officer Brown. His old heart couldn't take much more. He should have figured from his vampire research over many years that vampires are great deceivers.

Upon liftoff, the blood-shot eyed sheriff grabbed the chopper by the skid! With newfound supernatural strength, he pulled the wavering machine back down towards the roof!

"I need blood!" declared the undead sheriff as he continued to pin the helicopter down. "Don't leave me, Joshua. Give me your blood! Give me your blood!"

In complete fear, Officer Brown jiggled the helicopter from the sheriff's grip as he turned the chopper cyclic control stick in all directions and increased the height with the collective. The only thing he could manage to do was tilt the helicopter well enough for the spinning blade to hit fragments of the rooftop truss, some electrical units, and pipes.

With his last plea to God, the chopper miraculously freed! Upon circling the roof, it appeared that the bleached-skin sheriff lay stiff as a bump in the road because his head was decapitated. The chopper blade had ripped across the rooftop satellite and communications! A very sharp fragment of those pieces beheaded the burning undead sheriff. Officer Brown praised the Lord and was airborne.

He watched a car drive away from the precinct but was panicked into not further investigating anything more below even if it involved two of his favorite officers' safety. Vampires could fly too, as bats! Off he flew into the vibrant moonlight with a full tank of gas in the chopper. He figured that if his old pal Sheriff Edward Sherman got bitten, he was surely next for the same, shared crime against Sir Sange decades before too.

Chapter 5

Stolen Passion

Officer Bowie dropped off Officer Michelle Achebe at her home. They had a rule that until she introduced him as her boyfriend to her daughter, he would have to play it without a goodnight kiss. In other words, he needed to finalize his divorce before diving deeper into their relationship. He watched Officer Achebe's great big bubble butt shake with every step, the sweetest smelling butt seat sweat all up in her butt crack, all the way to the front door. She was undoubtedly one of the hottest moms in the city. "Hey, I'll pick you up at about 9:30 am. Good night now!"

"Stick around Theo; I'll give you a quick window show," stated Officer Achebe. She wanted to clarify to him that he was the guy she wanted, which avoided any further conversation about earlier tonight. "All of the neighbors across the street are asleep, so it'll be me from head to toe."

Officer Bowie did not quarrel with that, except that if he waited too late, he could fall asleep. He figured it would be about ten minutes from now since she probably had to say goodnight to her kid and freshen up. So, he drove off to the local liquor store and bought some peep show treats: A cup of coffee, a box of Lemon Heads and Baked Beans, peanuts, some bagged popcorn, and some napkins.

"Wow officer," said an unwelcome voice when he got to the liquor store, "you've got a sweet tooth tonight, or are you smoking a little marijuana these nights? Those are signs of the munchies."

Officer Bowie controllably approached the accented man. "Officer Prendergast, I would have never imagined running into your creepy ass here. Why are you still around town? You're from the county located on the other side of Skull Hill. The case closed hours ago. So, again why are you still here in my town?"

"I like it here because you have all of the prettiest women. I hoped to find a needy woman at the bar tonight. I'm all ears if you know somebody. Perhaps your sexy wife, Jill, is free? I have a good nose for finding needy women. I would savagely tear Jill up!"

"Fuck you."

"On second thought, I probably don't need your help. You're a cheating man, Officer Bowie. Tell me, officer. Is Officer Achebe a lively lover in the bed? I would presume; she has quite the physique. I would pay a hefty amount of money to sink my teeth into her titillating body."

Officer Bowie rushed to the visitor's face!

"Go on and strike me," requested Officer Prendergast. "You'll be arrested and placed in your jail! That would be the grandest scenario to have you removed from the public eye."

"I don't know what your deal is, but I know that you're not here to look for whores at some bar."

"Yes, I am."

"Give me one reason not to bash your face, Officer Prendergast! If I hear that you've come near my girl one time, you son of a bitch, I'll find you and beat the hell out of you. Now, get out of my town!"

"You're not a very nice person, sir. Did you just ask me to leave your town?"

"Did I stutter, you stupid nerd?"

"You're beneath me; in time, I will crush your spirit. Until then, watch yourself." Officer Prendergast left his basket of goods on the floor and instantly walked out of the store.

Blocks away, Officer Achebe walked upstairs to find that her daughter, Jenny, peacefully nestled in her bed. All was peaceful in the face of doom.

"Mom, I'm glad you're home."

"So am I," replied her mother. "I'm sorry; I thought you were asleep. We're going to talk about the stunt you pulled today; you skipped school. We'll talk tomorrow. So, you make sure that you come straight home after school."

"I got it, mom!" Jenny yelled. "I was trying to be nice. Dang mom, why are you so jittery? My friends and I suspect that something happened early Sunday morning. Nobody is telling us anything around here, but we know something occurred in the middle of the night. You know, mom, I'm starting to think that the reason nothing is being said or reported is because of the annual wrestling show coming is coming to town this weekend. Nobody wants to lose a profit at any cost, even over spilled blood! Mom, do not sell out."

"Girl, just make sure to have your dirty laundry downstairs by the morning. The washer has gone out; I need to make a trip to the laundromat."

"Don't try to sidetrack me, mother. Tell me that I'm lying, mother."

"Is that the kind of stuff you teens discuss down at Levi's Coffee Stop, a bunch of wacky conspiracies and anti-government propaganda? Everything is fine. Don't forget about your laundry. I'm going to turn in now. Goodnight."

Notably chilly in Jenny's room, her mother walked to the window and regrettably shut it. She plugged her nose, stepped over a pile of her daughter's dirty underclothing, walked out of that smelly room, and nearly shut the door.

The officer then took a warm bath, made herself a late snack, and relaxed on the living room couch. She set her alarm and placed her cellular phone on the coffee table next to her, as she figured if she fell asleep, her alarm clock would ring nearby. The television played at the lowest volume. Soon after, she dropped the remote control and fell asleep on the couch.

The chimes outside of Jenny's window ceased. Dense smog lingered outside of her window. Suddenly, the latch on the window pane unlocked. The window slowly opened, as a thick haze engulfed the room. A hideous bat with a near-human face slowly entered Jenny's bedroom in flight. It hovered over an open area at the foot of her bed. Then, the bat metamorphosed into a hauntingly smoothed man.

He fixed his eyes upon Jenny's satiable sunny aura, as she slept. He suddenly entered her mind with his telepathic gifts, where he found Jenny sitting at a pond. This nighttime marauder was not of this dimension; no dream had boundaries.

He did not say a word in her dream; only he sat and leaned over her. To Jenny, he was irresistible in her dream, as she urged to unbutton her shirt. Yet, she too was familiar and beautiful to him from her temples to her hips, but not enough to serve as more than food for thought. After getting his thrill of caressing her familiarity, he planned to suck her blood and keep her as one of his succubi. However, Jenny was a talker in her sleep and loudly moaned of delightfulness.

Suddenly, a looming shadow stood in the open doorway of Jenny's bedroom with a loaded pistol! "What in the hell is going on here? Who's there?"

Jenny quickly awoke and sat up! She moved her bedsheets back over her revealed body.

The vampire struck sight with Officer Achebe. "It is you! How fate has brought us together. You have such an uncanny resemblance to my once bride, centuries ago. We must be together. Come…"

"Officer Prendergast?" The officer whispered and fell into a sudden trance, under the dim room. She became speechless, as she was at Skull Hill. However, her will to resist was gone.

"Come to me," whispered the vampire.

Jenny climbed down from her bed and stood in front of her mother. "Wait for a second! Officer Prendergast, you followed me home? What are you doing here? Officer Prendergast?"

Her mother took a step towards him and dropped her pistol, as Jenny resisted.

"Come to me," demanded Officer Prendergast. He strained his eyes even so, as his mind control was too strong for Jenny's mother to resist his command. "Come… to me."

"Mom!" shouted Jenny. She suddenly was struck with some sense when she saw his lengthy fangs. She realized that the hot officer was none other than a real vampire! "Mom, don't go to him. Stop! Mom! Please! He's a vampire, mom! Snap out of it!"

"You get out of the way, little girl!" With his eyes fixed on her mother, the vampire waved one hand. Suddenly, Jenny went airborne and violently crashed into her dresser. "Come to me."

Jenny grabbed her mother's loaded pistol and aimed at the vampire. She fired a shot at him, but it disappeared upon impact with his body. There was no ricochet and no blood. The bullet simply vanished.

Officer Bowie was outside. He felt ripped off for not seeing a kinky window peep show from his partner. Then again, maybe Officer Achebe was exhausted tonight from overtime and probably fell asleep. Just as he was about to start his car, he heard a gunshot!

"What in the world?" He jumped out of his car and headed to the front door as if he was on duty. He pulled his gun out and kicked in the front door!

"Michelle?" He called her name a few times; he headed up the stairs to the bedrooms. She was not in her bedroom. He snuck to her daughter's bedroom. "Michelle? Jenny?"

"Help us!" screamed Jenny. She pointed to the masculine figure, which partially hid behind her mother at the window.

Officer Bowie turned on the bedroom light and aimed his gun. "Who the hell are you to be coming up in this house? By the way, you're under arrest because I am a cop!"

"Is that so?"

"That is so, you bloodshot- eyed chump." Officer Bowie pulled out his wallet and showed his badge. "You're trespassing. From the looks of it, I see there was an altercation with the young lady too. Michelle, I want you to slowly back away from the intruder."

Jenny yelled, "Officer Bowie, he is a real a vampire!"

"What? Is that some kind of new street gang name or something? Yo', I'm a werewolf, yo! I be' illing."

"No! I swear it that he's a real vampire!"

Officer Bowie puckered his lips. "Get the hell out of here with all that, girl. If he's a vampire, then I am an invisible man. You can see me, can't you? Come on."

Officer Achebe remained with her back to Officer Bowie, as the wind shuffled her silky white nightwear to the side. She and the intruder remained unmoved.

"I don't have all day!" Officer Bowie was impatient. "Michelle, you know that I have the quickest draw in these parts. You're going to have to trust me. Move away from –"

It was the masculine figure that purposely moved from around Jenny's mother so that Officer Bowie could positively identify him.

"Officer Prendergast!" Officer Bowie was grateful in that second that it was him. "Dude, I hope you understand how you messed up tonight. I am going to enjoy beating you up."

The vampire reached for Officer Achebe's neck and kissed her there. He then took his hand with extraordinarily extended nails and felt her down to her hip. She was in a trance and silently stood still, as Officer Prendergast moved his hands to eclipse her soft buttocks completely. He slowly massaged her and softly ran his thumb up the lower portion of her spine.

"Mom!" cried Jenny. She stayed behind Officer Bowie.

"What in the hell," said Officer Bowie. "Do you have her drugged or something? Michelle, can you hear me? I cannot believe that you just groped her in front of her teenage daughter! Have you no moral compass?"

"I will do far more things to her in, which you could not imagine; I cannot share in the presence of a minor. Now, what are you going to do about this boggle? I haven't got all nightfall, as the morning is near."

"Well, shit. I guess it's time to kick your ass."

Officer Bowie shoved his girlfriend to the side and stood face to face with the vampire. Jenny kneeled beside her mother and tried to awaken her from the vampire's sensual trance.

"Trust me, officer tough guy. You do not want to engage me." The vampire controlled his rage and lifted his chin high. Then he lowered his head and strained an eye at Officer Bowie.

The officer bumped his gums about kicking this and kicking that. Frankly, the threats were entertainment to the vampire, who could have quickly shut Officer Bowie's mouth and broken him in half.

"Are you all talk, or are you going to... so-called, kick my ass, little man?"

"Did you just call me a little man?"

"Yes, I did, as in size matters." The vampire lusted over Officer Achebe and smirked.

Officer Bowie quickly placed his gun in his hip holster and then socked the masculine figure in the face! However, upon assessment of his bloody knuckles afterward, he was sure it was appropriate to cry. He dropped to his knees to nurse his swollen hand!

"Now," said the vampire, "let that be a warning to all of you. In exchange for sparing your lives, I will take what I have awakened for all of these centuries. Oh, I sense that at least one of you is confused. Then let me be clear that I killed an Officer Prendergast in another county, so I just put on his uniform and put on a good show at the cave. My assurance to you is that my real name is Sir Sange!"

"No, wait!" Jenny reached for her mother, as the officer mystically gravitated towards the uninvited intruder. There she stood in a trance, face to face with him.

Officer Bowie slowly turned towards a mirror on the wall to his right. His experience of vampires came from movies. To his dismay, Sir Sange was not in the reflection of the mirror; only his partner was. The tiniest hairs on the back of Officer Bowie's neck suddenly stiffened, as a cold chill ran up his back!

"Please, do not take her!" Officer Bowie grimly pleaded as he backed away in absolute fear. Jenny tried to grab him from the floor to run, but her legs failed with a shiver. He begged and cried out, "Michelle, please snap out of it! Wake up!"

"I'm going to take Michelle away with me now," stated the calm vampire, "and there is not a damn thing that either of you can do about it. Now, move out of my way!"

The vampire violently shoved both Jenny and Officer Bowie to the side, as he led his victim down the stairs and out the front door.

Both, the off duty police officer and daughter, conjured up their strength and ran to the front door. Jenny grabbed her cell phone on the way out. No matter how much they called for Officer Achebe in the late hours of darkness, there was no response from anybody.

Officer Bowie ran to his car. Jenny followed him.

"This is Officer Bowie," he radioed the police station from his car. "Is anyone there? Does anyone read me? Hello? Hello! Is anybody there?"

"Hello," responded a familiar voice, although it wasn't the voice of any of the emergency dispatchers. It was a bit distant, as static filled the connection.

"Get me the sheriff now," demanded Officer Bowie. "It's an emergency!"

"I'm afraid that the sheriff is dead," replied the voice.

"What do you mean that the sheriff is dead? Who is this?"

"This is Officer Joshua Brown."

"You fly the chopper for the precinct," Officer Bowie recognized. "What are you doing intercepting the department's emergency line? It sounds as if you're flying. What is going on?"

"Yes, I fly the chopper. Who am I talking with?"

"Sir, this is Officer Bowie, and I'm with a civilian. I don't know what is going on around here, but you won't believe the Halloween shit I came across tonight! We are in some danger here, sir!"

"Try me."

"Sir, I just encountered a real vampire!"

Officer Brown shook his head. "Listen to me. Do not, I repeat, do not return to the precinct. The vampire you speak of has turned those on the late shift into pale monsters as well, who feed upon human blood."

"Get in the car," demanded Officer Bowie to Jenny. She hopped into the passenger seat; he sat it in the driver's seat. They locked their doors!

"Watch your back," warned Officer Brown. "We have no idea what's going to happen. You'll need to stay away from everyone until daylight. You cannot trust anyone, you know. I made the same mistake with the sheriff tonight; he certainly almost got me. I'm telling you, we just don't know what or who we're dealing with."

"I'll tell you who. It's a bloody vampire that calls himself Sir Sange! Then he kidnapped this girl's mother, Officer Michelle Achebe. We got to do something about that!"

Officer Brown swallowed. "You've met Sir Sange face to face and lived?"

"Yes," answered Jenny. "He spared our life for my mother's life!"

"That sounds about right." Officer Brown figured.

Officer Bowie stated, "You act as if you know of this creature already."

"The sun will be rising soon," stated Officer Brown. He did not want to frighten Jenny with the truth that her mother was good as dead, nor discuss his past with crossing the very same evil. He added, "Anything that you can recall about how to kill a vampire from any number of monster movies will be a plus. Be ready to arm yourself. Hopefully, we can convene at noon on channel 8?"

"Can you come down here and pick us up now?" asked Jenny. "I don't feel safe around here! I don't feel safe! Are you near?"

"What's your 20?" asked Officer Bowie. "It doesn't feel safe down here."

"I am not too far from the city," answered the lonely cop in the chopper. He levitated a few miles from the city. "I'm afraid that I cannot return to the city at this time. I have eyes on several bats circling above you, perhaps watching or feeding. They're nocturnal beings, so they'll be gone by the morning. I say the best of luck to you two tonight. For now, you two get out of sight for a good four hours! I need to get out of sight, as I'm afraid even being airborne is not safe; I'm going off-walkie. Tomorrow, noon, you both be on channel 8 for instructions. I need to find a plan. Good luck to you both."

"Call the National Guard or something!"

"The communication towers located atop the precinct have been compromised, where it only allows for some nearer connection. No phones or Internet work. Only short-range radio frequencies on talkies or Citizens' Band seem to work within the range of our city."

"Copy that," said Officer Bowie. He slowly drove away from the Achebe residence with his vehicle lights off. Cautiously, he watched for any signs of any monsters on the prowl. "If they are watching from above, we need to be under something for the night."

Jenny was scared and tired. "No, I think we should leave the city!"

"We'll be the only car on the road; we'd be an easy target," said the officer.

"Turn over there in that driveway," instructed Jenny. She told Officer Bowie to back his car into the covered carport of none other than Demarcus Peter's home. She had never officially dated the young stud, but she had been by his home for a house party or two to wall out.

"Isn't this the home where Demarcus Peeler, the high school quarterback lives? Leave it up to Michelle's kid to have an interest in the best of the best. And I suppose that you wouldn't be able to tell me how you knew those carport lights wouldn't come on? We could have been in the spotlight for all of those creatures that lurk in the sky."

Jenny thought back about the recent conversation she had with Demarcus. Just a few weeks ago, it was Demarcus, some friends, and Jenny that stood under the very same carport, quietly drinking in the dark and making out after a house party. She recalled that Demarcus mentioned the carport lights did not work because his dad cut the wires to avoid his mom from catching him sneaking off to bars late at night. Since his dad refused alcohol treatment or counseling help, Demarcus' mom kicked his dad out a couple of weeks ago. So, his dad took the old 1980 Caprice, loaded with alcohol, and declared that he would find fortune someday even if he had to rob a bank. That unwelcomed lunatic never returned as promised and never would.

Jenny nodded, sat back in her seat, and quietly whimpered. "This is just the house of somebody I trust and admire. I guess, for now, we wait for sunrise to rescue my mother. Do you mind if I eat some of your Lemon Heads or Baked Beans and maybe of the bag of popcorn on the floor? I don't even care if the coffee is cold; I hope you don't mind me drinking it."

"Have at it," whispered Officer Bowie. He watched the hungry girl eat the treats he intended to eat while he was going to watch her mother put on a dirty window show for him. He chuckled for a second at that, though. Then it went away; his spirit crushed. He stared out into the darkness through is his car windows. Everything seemed very peaceful in the face of doom.

Yet, neither she nor the police officer intended to sleep or make a peep of noise.

Chapter 6

The Alliance

Suddenly a familiar and loud sports car roared up the street and aggressively parked in front of Officer Bowie's car. As if it weren't enough noise pollution with the liveliest and most expensive muffler installed on a vehicle, the driver of his prized possession slammed his breaks from a house away. His tires ripped the asphalt with a squeal that was louder and longer than a Killer Whale's mating call.

Officer Bowie was awakened to bright, early morning sunshine by the awful sound and smell of burned rubber. "What in the blue hell is going on?"

"Dude, what do we have here?" It was none other than Jessup Jackson in all his glory, with two of his obnoxious, school pals. There he stood and pointed into Officer Bowie's car. "Is that Jenny? That is Jenny! She's a freak! Look at her with the old geezer! Oh, wait! That's not Demarcus' dad. He's old, but that's not him! Did you two have a little too much to drink last night and pull into the wrong driveway? Let me get some panty pictures! Jenny is too sexy!"

Jenny angrily awakened and opened her car door, as did Officer Bowie.

"You guys are idiots!" Officer Bowie pulled out his wallet and badge. He held them high for the school jocks to see. "We are in grave danger."

Jenny added, "You are totally out of line, Jessup! Delete all the pictures, you go to the front door, and have Demarcus come outside. We need to talk to him right now!"

"Okay… Damn girl, don't be so pushy. We were just playing." Jessup waved his hand. "Gross! Your breath smells like straight shit! You need to brush those teeth before class today."

"There's no way in hell I'm going to school!"

"Wow!" Jessup was impressed. "You're finally turning into a bad girl. You want to skip school than Demarcus isn't the guy you want to be dating. Look no further than I!"

Officer Bowie hastily stepped around his car and right up to Jessup. "Go over there and knock on that door. Get the other kid outside as she asked, or I'm going to smash your head in!"

"Settle down," relieved Jessup. He went to knock on the front door.

After Officer Bowie and Jenny explained to Demarcus and his high school goons what they experienced last night, everyone stopped to figure out what to do. Besides Officer Theodore Bowie and Officer Joshua Brown, the rest of the police force was not to be trusted.

"Hmm, that's funny." Demarcus looked out the window and noticed that his mother's car parked in front of the house. "She isn't usually home on Mondays."

Demarcus crept upstairs and lightly knocked on his mother's bedroom door. She did not respond, so he cautiously entered.

"Mom, did you forget about work today or oversleep?"

His mother did not respond. She lay there, as stiff as a log.

Demarcus looked around the room, and suspected alcohol may have been in play. His drunken mother had passed out and a little pale. "Mom, you need to wake up for work. You're going to be late. You don't have to drink your life away because dad left!."

He shook her by the shoulders. Was she dead? Just as he was about to believe so, he noticed two deep bites on her neck! His mother quickly grabbed his arm, pulled him close, and opened her mouth as if she was about to bite him!

"All I want is your blood!" Demarcus' mother begged, "Give me your blood!"

"Get away from her!" shouted Officer Bowie. He had booked up the stairs just in time and yanked the bedroom curtains open so that the sunlight fixed on Demarcus' mother.

"No!" screamed Demarcus' mother, as she let go of her son's arm to block the brilliant sunlight. She revealed fangs as long as a wolf's and bloodshot eyes of red! She madly hissed at the bright sunshine! She ignited in flames with her legs dangling out the bedsheets, while her flimsy polyester collapsed in a twisted wringing of her sweaty sagging busts because both of her fleshless hands melded to her burning skull. With the last torturous plea for help, she yelled, "Demarcus, tell them to close the curtain! Close the curtain, please! I am your mother! It hurts! It hurts!"

"Close the fucking curtains!" shouted Demarcus, as he stumbled to the floor and watched his poor burning mother erupt in flames in her bed! His friends pinned him down as he questioned what was going on. "Somebody help her! Get off of me!"

"Help me, Demarcus…"

"Didn't you hear what we said downstairs?" Jenny ran into Demarcus' arms. "That was not your mother! She got bitten by a vampire! I'm sorry. She's gone! I'm so sorry."

"No!" Demarcus did the impossible and threw nine touchdowns in a game last year to break the school record, but he could not help his mother. There she was, a mouth retainer and hair net upon ashes on crispy sheets.

"I'm sorry, kid," said Officer Bowie.

Demarcus angrily stood to his feet. He looked at the officer. "You son of a bitch, you killed my mother! That's what you did. I'm going to kill your ass!"

"She was already dead!" screamed Jenny, who intercepted him. "She was bitten probably last night by a vampire! Demarcus, she was not your mother this morning. That wasn't her! Look at her! She had fangs and was going to kill you!"

"This isn't real," said Jessup. "Oh my god, this cannot be real! Do vampires exist? What do we do now? How do we stop this? We need answers, man! We need answers now!"

Officer Bowie tried to calm everyone. "I think we need to find the main host again, but we need to kill Sir Sange this time. That's how we save everyone. Yeah, that's how they do it in movies."

"Sir Sange?" Demarcus shook his head in denial. "He's like the main vampire! He's like the leader of all the vampires. And what do you mean this time?"

Jenny said, "He was in my house and took my mother away."

"He took her, but he didn't kill her," Jessup added. "Yeah, Jenny, your mom is hotter than Demarcus', but not by much. I've seen pictures of your mom in local magazines, but today seeing Demarcus' mom in the slutty lingerie was hot! I mean, not hot due to the flames she went up in, but hot like sexy?"

"Are you serious right now, Jessup?" Demarcus looked at Jessup. He couldn't bring himself to punch him out. Jessup was his best friend since elementary, even despite the saying that he couldn't find his ass with both hands and a flashlight. "Jessup, will you just shut the hell up? I just lost my damn mom; I can't handle this shit!"

"I'm sorry, bro. I didn't mean to be insensitive. Why'd I even say that?"

Officer Bowie whispered, "Seriously, I would've punched the mother fucker out."

"Alright, boys," said Jenny, as she looked at the alarm clock on the dresser. "Officer Bowie, we need to contact your friend in the helicopter soon. Maybe he can help us? He said to reach him on Channel 8."

"Until then, let's all gather at Levi's Coffee Stop while there is still sunlight," instructed Officer Bowie. "Just like you witnessed here, I want everyone in here to be careful when you go home or try to find friends that may not have gotten bit. Also, everything you know about killing vampires might be your best weapon, from holy water and garlic to wooden stakes and crucifies. Take a good look at her. I hope to God that you all have faith because that's the only way any of those weapons will be effective. Isn't that how it works? With that said, let's meet in two hours at Levi's Coffee Stop."

On the way out of the house, Jessup said to Jenny and Demarcus, "That's just great. I'll be the first one to hold up a cross and get the hell bitten out of me. I haven't gone to church or practiced any kind of faith since the fourth grade. How was I supposed to know that all that spirit stuff was real? Faith is a bitch, man."

"I say we just go straight to Levi's," Demarcus said to everybody. "Hey, we pay for text messaging. So, if my boys don't respond for hours, then I know they're dead."

"What if they're in class and can't answer the text?" Jenny worried. "What if nobody was affected like we are thinking and our classmates went into school?"

"Then they should answer," answered Jessup. "Whoever doesn't check their text messages, at least every hour, is a freaking geek and deserves what's coming to them."

"Even I second that," said Officer Bowie. "What? Let's roll, people!"

Jenny thought Officer Bowie was kind of cool.

Headed to Levi's Coffee Stop, both Officer Bowie and Demarcus steered their car through the desolate streets of San De Juan. There was a ghostly feel to the town, as most businesses remained unusually closed. The typical school and transit buses were absent. Fewer businesspeople walked up and down the boulevard than usual, the morning rush hour traffic was uncommonly light, and there wasn't a homeless person in sight.

As soon as they arrived at Levi's Coffee Stop, Officer Bowie quickly walked up to the glass door and banged for anyone to open up. It was the owner, Levi Franklin, who came to the door.

"What now?" Levi questioned. "What do you want, cop? I have paid for all of my outstanding tickets! Why don't you step off and give a brother a chance to breathe?"

"What!"

"Oh, I've got it," said Levi. "You're here for the lazy employee I recently hired! Well, he's thirty minutes late to work this morning; I don't have a good phone number for him. I think the guy walked off the job yesterday, now that I think of it. He must've left when all the kids headed out to talk to that police."

"Open this door, Levi."

"We're not quite open yet, so you'll have to be patient for the powdered donuts!"

Officer Bowie pulled his gun out. "Man, if you don't open this door!"

Levi unlocked the door. The officer and the teenagers rushed into his restaurant!

"Lock the door," demanded Officer Bowie. "Somebody open all of the curtains!"

"What is the meaning of this?"

Officer Bowie shoved Levi into the bright light coming through the window and aimed his gun at the owner's head.

"Hey!" Levi sat on his boney buttocks with his hands out. "Whoa! That's police brutality. What's the meaning of pushing me, an older man, to the floor like that? Help! Somebody help me! Don't shoot! Somebody record this shit on their phone! What did I do?"

Jenny held onto Levi's arm and gently lifted him from the floor. "He's okay because he's with me. You can put the gun away, officer."

Officer Bowie put his gun away on his merit and said, "We have a problem. We need to develop a plan, but it's going to take a few good men and women to make this work."

Excitedly, those in the restaurant rejoiced to see that a few cars began to pull up the restaurant. High school punks and thugs, some players and the clueless, jocks, and the adventurous were allowed into the restaurant. The excitement quickly tapered down, though, as the new crowd danced to no music and smoked a lot of weed. Others carried on with conversations about humping this girl or that guy, threatened the owner to make cheese sandwiches, and acted like a bunch of spring break, boob jiggling, and beer chugging, territorial gangsters.

"Not a nerd insight," whispered the officer. "We really could've used brains for this situation. I guess we'll just put all of these clowns on the front line."

A cross-eyed, 350-pound football player for the school, who caressed a ditzy cheerleader's ear with his wet thumb, spoke out. "Hey, what is the meaning of calling us here like this? If you're not giving out free beer, what's the meaning of all this skipping class?"

When Paul Glasgow spoke, everybody listened. So, the restaurant was quiet.

Demarcus stepped up to address everyone. He had the respect from everyone in school, as he was the starting quarterback for the town's high school football team. "If you all have not noticed this morning, the population around the city has dramatically changed. There are fewer people. My friends and I have come across something that, when I tell you, you won't believe me. We need your help! We cannot do this without each one of you."

"Spit it out!" shouted Paul Glasgow. "What do you need help with, little buddy? You're my quarterback for the high school football team. As your Left Guard, you know that I've always got you. I got you, buddy! What do you need? What's up?"

"We're dealing with vampires!"

Levi spat out his gum and his dentures! "Have you lost your mind?"

"What? Get the fuck out of here with that bull jive!" Paul led the numerous laughs and put-downs at Demarcus. "Demarcus, you have been hit too many times in the pocket during football games! You need to see a doctor! Somebody turn up the jukebox and let's party up in here! I need another freaky girl on my other lap! Somebody, please pass me a joint!"

Everybody opposed they laughed at Demarcus. He and his vampire slayers stood there with no extra help. The jukebox got plugged in, and hip hop blared throughout the restaurant. People smoked weed, ate food, freaked one another to the music, talked about one another, and had a good time.

"You're a few fries short of a happy meal there, Demarcus!" Levi laughed himself into a near stroke, as he strutted around his refurbished jukebox. He just shook his head and thanked Demarcus for telling fairy tales that got him the unusually crowded business today! He scrambled eggs, tossed some hotcakes, flung plates of food to people's tables, and collected money. "I got coffee! Who wants bacon? Who wants grits? That'll be nineteen dollars. That comes to twenty-eight dollars and ten cents! That's a nice tip, thank you. Would you like some pecan pie?"

The restaurant boomed, but nothing prepared anyone inside for the loudest backfire from a car out front that pulled up or the screeching of tires from monster trucks and cars that followed. All of the fun in the restaurant was short-lived. To the surprise of the vampire slayers and the obnoxious, near dropouts, several enormous men and women stepped from busted cars and giant trucks with splattered guts and stood at the door of Levi's Coffee Stop. The size of those grunting individuals put every jock and badass in the restaurant in check.

The buzz-cut man in front, who squeezed out from a bruised police car with busted out headlights and blood over the hood, had biceps the size of a thirteen-sized bowling ball and an emotionless face with a humongous steel jaw. He walked by all of the giants and stood at the door. With his large combat boot, he kicked open the door and led his group of titans into the restaurant! Their eyes fixed on Levi.

"We would like some breakfast right now."

Levi gulped. "Do you have money?"

The enormous bodybuilder reached behind the jukebox and ripped the power cord out of the wall. The restaurant fell silent.

Jenny, not only noticed blood on their clothing, but she saw that some of them had big guns in their hands.

The big, furious, enormously unreal-sized, buzz-cut man moaned. He stared down Levi and dug in his pocket. He suddenly flung out a bunch of twenty-dollar bills over the counter.

"You all come in and have a seat. Welcome to Levi's Coffee Stop. I've never seen you any of you around these parts. Where are you decent folks from?"

All of the scared high school students jumped out of their seats. The grunting titans sat down in those chairs and ate the food from those plates.

"We need more food!" shouted one of the enormous guys. He chewed into the plate!

Jessup asked one of his close friends, "Do you know who he looks like?"

"Excuse me," said Officer Bowie to the buzz-cut titan. "I can see that you're hungry by the way you slurp down those cakes, but I noticed that you drove up in a beat-up police car. Did you all come from the police station up on the hill?"

"What's it to you?"

"I'm a cop, brother." Officer Bowie showed his badge.

The buzz-cut man speedily jumped from his table, grabbed Officer Bowie by the collar, spun him down to the table, and shouted, "Give me the stake, Rhonda! Can a man just sit down and eat without some blood-sucking, flying rat in a uniform interrupting?"

Rhonda, also known as Big Momma Brown, if recognizable through the bloody makings and town apparel on television, got up from the adjacent table. She was an enormous woman, comparable to an adult rhino in size, as she took up two chairs for each butt cheek. She pulled a wooden stake from her purse and handed it to the buzz-cut man. "Don't be calling me Rhonda in public!"

"Wait!" screamed Jenny. "Please stop! He's not a vampire! He's in the daylight coming from the window. We all are! He's not a vampire! None of us are vampires!"

"The light… Yeah, that makes sense." The buzz-cut man shoved the police officer to another table. "I'm sorry. I got to be more careful."

"You got that right," said Officer Bowie. He put his gun away. "You would not have succeeded in killing me without losing your balls."

Jessup then remembered. "You're the wrestler! That's right! You're all scheduled to entertain us at the biggest wrestling event all year, this weekend!"

Demarcus recognized and pointed to the buzz-cut wrestler. "You're Lumberjack Jones, the Pro Wrestling Heavyweight Champion of the World! And her over there, that's Big Momma Brown without the costume!"

Jessup blushed, for he had a thing for Big Momma Brown. However, Jenny was there, so he turned to look out the front window to hide his hard-on.

"You came across the vampires," said Officer Bowie. "Look, we could use your help."

"I don't think we have a choice," replied Lumberjack. "These monsters are everywhere. Some of us got snatched from the freeway last night, trying to leave here. These things are in all the nearby counties. Our best chance to get them is during the day, but there are so many of them. They have an army; we have this. I think our chances of survival are slim."

"Maybe not," said Officer Bowie. "We met the host last night, Sir Sange. If we get him, the others should go away or die, just like in the movies."

"You're going off of a movie to kill these things?" Miss Brown chuckled. "And isn't some kind of vampire a tale, made-for-movie, monster? He's not real. We're simply in the last days!"

"Hear me out," said Officer Bowie. "I know what I'm saying. I've seen the fangs, and I've seen what the bite marks on the neck mean. It means undead! Somebody in old novels or even Hollywood based on someone real! You can twist that any way you want to, but I know what I've seen, as well as yourself. You thought I was one of those things and wanted to take a stake to me. If it walks like a duck, it's a duck. I'm telling you that Sir Sange is a real vampire!"

"Can we call your friend now?" asked Jenny. "It's a little early, but we need to rescue my mother. Time is not on our side."

So, as everyone ate breakfast and listened, Officer Bowie and a few wrestlers went to his car and called the chopper on CB, as arranged on Channel 8.

"Breaker 1-9, Officer Brown, come in," said Officer Bowie. "Joshua, are you there - copy?"

"Affirmative... Copy that 10-2," replied the voice in static. "This is Josh."

"What's your 20?"

"I'm holding steady above the police station," answered Officer Brown. "I studied various places around town all morning. It would appear that the concentration of bats lingered above here all night. I have a hunch that the host, the main vampire, is here. Wait, somebody is crawling across the helicopter pad! He appears to be burning up in the sunlight, with what looks to be a rocket launcher on his back! What is he doing? Oh dear god, he's a sacrifice to the damned to be out in the sun! I got to get out of range!"

The line turned into static as an explosion echoed through the city. Everybody witnessed a helicopter explode and descend from the police station. There was a smaller explosion of smoke that appeared on the rooftop of the precinct, also.

Officer Bowie realized now that Officer Joshua Brown tried to warn him that the primary host, Sir Sange, was up there in the precinct! "We have to save Michelle tonight!"

"Who is Michelle?"

"She was my partner," said Officer Bowie, "and the young lady's mother inside Levi's."

"Sounds like she was more than your partner," said Miss Brown. "You love her, don't you? I wish I had a chance at love. We might as well fight for dignity, as well to live. We have beaten a few of the creatures, but we need more hands because the bullets aren't killing them. If we want to get out of this town alive, I think that we should help you."

"What if we defeat this Sir Sange and nothing ends?" asked Lumberjack. "Do we know that he's the key to all of this?"

"What's the option for us? Keep on randomly fighting until we lose in numbers and die off?" Officer Bowie stood front and center. "We're not going to be able to hide for much longer, especially during the nights. We have an alliance right now if we can join up. Daytime is our best friend, so we need to kill him right now!"

"I think that he is right," said Miss Brown. "The policeman said there was a person that came to the landing pad and caught fire before shooting him out of the air. I think we should go right now and round up some of those kids inside the restaurant to go kill Sir Sange right now."

That sounded fantastic and maybe foolproof, but only a handful of high school jocks and wrestlers teamed. Paul Glasgow, the biggest bully in high school, still was not one to join. He made that clear over the loud, restarted music that played from the jukebox.

"If I'm going out," Paul playfully declared, "it'll be with booze and bitches and not with some fantasy-driven, bull jive! I don't believe in any vampire nonsense. Do you guys take me for a fool? Do you take these people in here for some chumps? If we go up to that precinct, the sheriff is going to arrest us and send most of us home to our parents! Perhaps we'll all be suspended from school? I have a football scholarship to an outstanding college to protect, so I'm not going to allow any of you to mess that up!"

"You're skipping class right now," added Jenny.

Paul addressed Demarcus and Jessup. "And you two have a crush on that lippy bitch? Good luck with that! She's not even worth it. I've had my shot with her. She is overrated, just like my dad said her slutty mother was."

"That's crossing the line!" Officer Bowie shouted.

"Fuck you, cop. Have your wife come to my house for a real man."

Demarcus and Jessup held the police officer off. "He's a minor. It's just words."

"Screw you, Paul." Jenny flipped him off.

"You say that this vampire has a thirst for blood?" Paul spoke to those who joined Demarcus and Jessup. He sexually looked Jenny up and down. "Do you know what I got an itching for?"

Jenny added, "Yes. You got an itch because you got a venerable disease!"

"If I do, I got it from your whore of a mom! What kind of vampire would want to touch that dirty bitch?" Paul turned his back on Demarcus and friends, who walked out of the restaurant, and shouted to Levi, "Right now, I got a thirst for another glass of beer! Aye Levi, give me another refill on the dark brew!"

By Ashaki Boelter

Chapter 7

The Advantage

Overwhelmingly patience was the precise narrative of the starved vampire that had retired sleep after many years, as his hunger for endless love and unsurmountable blood was unbearable for the immediate wake of dawn. He had defeated the surveilling chopper by an unthinkably honorable suicide and forced the surrender of his deputy, a pawn for a queen; instead, revenge that somebody that once conquered him decades ago by the name of Joshua Brown was gone. The damned never forgot. He was not fooled or ruled by such impotence that wisdom supplied it was best to conquer him in the daylight. This time around, he schemed to use the presence of light as his tamed and contorted advantage and not as a weapon of humankind or divine holiness.

The centuries-old, gothic nobleman marveled at the old architecture of the precinct upon the hill, his newly dark tomb, an oddly familiar construction of his Romanian land. Quite intrigued, Sir Sange slowly paced throughout the darkened office once owned by the sheriff. It was his new castle now, as a spell-bound mortician and assistants from the neighboring morgue spent the night delivering caskets and boxes for those he eternally turned.

Sir Sange's casket had since been destroyed in Transylvania decades ago. His new bed was tailored especially for familiarity, which sat in the corner wherein his anticipated bride, Officer Michelle Achebe, currently slept under his spell. All of the other caskets throughout the precinct contained resting vampires during daylight, in a state of undead sleep with their eyes open.

"We shall rise again!" Sir Sange declared. He then swooped down to his victim's ear and whispered, "Once I make you my bride tonight, we shall delight our thirst in the remnants of this town, and then return to Transylvania in numbers. We will control the world!"

Just as Sir Sange's blackened heart propelled to kiss her upon the lips, he turned to the sound of a door opening. Somebody had entered the precinct through a side door with a key and without invitation. He slowly stood up straight and looked peculiar towards his office door. He listened, as he smelled fresh blood and lots of it.

"Alright, everybody needs to watch your ass in here and not get bit," warned Lumberjack Jones, as he held the side door open. Everyone had a wooden stake in-hand. "I know that these vampires are supposed to be asleep in the daytime, but I don't trust everything that I've read. One other thing is that Officer Bowie said that his girlfriend is the only female officer with short hair above her shoulders, so if you cross her, you don't want to stab Jenny's mother."

"She may not have been bitten yet," said Jenny. "Sange could've bitten her last night when he kidnapped her, but he didn't. So, she may still be normal for whatever the reason."

"I don't care how fine your mother is… because if she has gotten bit," whispered Jessup, "I'm stabbing that fine bitch. I'm sorry, Jenny, but that's what's up."

Demarcus shoved Jessup. "Don't be insensitive. Stay focused."

"If you get bitten, I'm also taking you out, Demarcus."

"Come on! Stay focused." Officer Bowie shook his head to show a hopeful sign of solidarity with Jenny, but deep down inside, he shared the same sentiment, as did the rest. He thought, "She'd better be human or else."

"I don't know if I can do this," said a worried teenage girl who grabbed Demarcus' arm. "I should've gone home to at least check. Maybe everyone was fine? After all, my parents own a lot of guns. I'm scared! Please, stay close to me, Demarcus."

Jenny ripped the girl away from Demarcus and replied, "Don't be stupid. Our phones didn't work; neither do guns against those things. I saw that with my own eyes!"

"How dare you grab my arm, bitch? Who do you think you are?"

"Ladies, please!" Demarcus separated them, as the angry teen lingered closer to him despite Jenny being there. "Keep moving."

Jenny held onto Demarcus's hand. She victoriously smiled back at the challenger.

Out of the ten antsy high schoolers that snuck down the hallway, none of their phones appeared to be in service as of this morning. Nobody in the entire area, which included the professional wrestlers, had a signal to draw from since the officer's chopper damaged the Base Transceiver Station for cell phone signals, located on the precinct roof earlier.

So, instead of going home and finding their families in a gruesome and undead way, the brave and assembled group of jocks and professional wrestlers, led by Officer Bowie, honed in to kill Sange. That way, once he was dead, everything he impacted would be reversed.

However, because of their emotions, numbers, and muscle, they had not truly strategized or thought out any alternative options if such a tactic failed; they never accounted for Sange's magnificent brilliance and resilience of living for centuries. Every single person had erred in the past and present of ending his reign of terror. In other words, they walked right into his trap.

There they stood and blankly stared at a locked storm door, the entrance to the administration offices. That door was usually never closed and, for that matter, locked. Officer Bowie tried several keys he had in his pocket in the door; none of them fit. He turned to the group and quietly signaled to turn around and go back the way they came, as there was another entrance from outside of the precinct.

Lumberjack Jones shook his head and puckered his lips. "Let me tell you something, brother. If we can get a few tough guys to join me in ramming or kicking that door down, we'll be through there in no time."

"Impossible," said Officer Bowie. "That storm door is bullet-proofed and a solid five feet of titanium, designed to keep prisoners from any outbreak or any groups from getting in. It's one of a kind, as this precinct was once a homemade bomb shelter."

"That's funny," said Jessup, "because I always thought this place was more like a castle on top of a hill with great accommodations. I've been here a few times. How old is this place anyways, Officer Bowie?"

"Excuse me!" Jenny shouted. She was bumped in the shoulder by the girl that tried to come onto Demarcus a minute ago.

"Don't get in my way, then."

"How dare you, bitch!" Jenny prepared to go upside that girl's head with her fist.

Demarcus pulled Jenny away, so she would not attack the teenager. Not only was that smart to help Jenny keep her strength for battle later, that was probably a significant coincidence of events, as the flirtatious female shoved her way towards the opposite end of the hallway. It was a very dark lobby down there.

"What's down there?" asked Lumberjack Jones. Nobody paid him any attention, and he suddenly forgot what he asked. "You've got to be kidding me! Shake what your momma gave you! Who is that girl?"

Jessup nearly fainted when she passed him.

Guys noticed the strange flirtatious girl's cut-off baby blue shorts, as her wobbly buttocks moved like two thawed and fatty pot roasts, side-by-side and asynchronously ground on two cheese graters. She walked past everyone as if she was all that.

"I swear that I'm not looking!" Demarcus declared. He turned around.

That flirtatious girl turned around at the end of the hall where the dark lobby was. Then she revealed her sinisterly black heart when she smiled and showed her sharp fangs!

"She's a vampire!" Jenny shouted.

The female cackled and hissed at the wrestlers. "Get out of my way!" She opened her mouth so wide that an entire human head could fit inside in one swallow. "I shall see to it that…"

Everybody immediately moved towards the locked storm door at the end of the hallway, feared for their lives! The vampire stopped at the side door and especially stared stained red eyes of hell's fire into Jenny. She opened the side door that they all walked in to get into the hallway and continued, "…you and he will be my master's satisfaction to his thirst for blood."

The vampire exited the hallway and quickly slammed the side door shut behind her!

"Let's get the hell out of here!" A wrestler shouted. "The side door still works!"

The hesitated wrestlers and football jocks jumped to the side door and began to kick and push at it to open it. Unfortunately, other unrested vampires that were outside the hall pushed a vehicle sideways against the door!

"It looks like there's a car up against the door," said one of the high school football players, who peeked through the slightly opened side door. "A car is sideways against the door! We're trapped!"

"Oh yeah," remembered Lumberjack Jones, "what's down the other end of the hallway?"

"Oh, hell, no!" answered another wrestler. "It's pitch black down there."

Officer Bowie added, "It's the lobby and the front door."

Lumberjack Jones asked, "Do you think it's a trap or ambush? It's like too easy to just walk down there in the dark."

"We got weapons and stakes," said Jessup.

"Yeah, like I want to be the one to test our luck first!" Lumberjack Jones was a tall and muscular wrestler, but even he doubted the dark hallway for an escape. "Somebody else could've taken a swipe at the female vampire a second ago."

Another wrestler replied, "Well, you're the leader around here. You're the Heavyweight Champion! Why didn't you take a swipe?"

"Why should I? I'm the money maker for this company! If something happened to me, all of you would get a pay cut because of the lack of fans!"

"You arrogant son of a bitch, you're not that talented, Lumberjack! You only got one good move!"

The wrestlers cursed and argued as to why none of them had the guts to stab that vampire. They had regularly jumped off turnbuckles and flew at least from ten feet in the air onto tables, hit one another with chairs, and jumped through glass windows in hardcore matches, but when it came to jumping, just one vampire to save their lives, they had no guts. After all, it was what everyone had come to the station to do; they all had wooden stakes!

"Man," screamed a newer wrestler, "don't yell at me! I didn't sign a contract for this! I'm just an entertainer! I'm not a killer! I'm certainly not some kind of vampire slayer!"

"You're a coward!" Another wrestler grabbed that wrestler and began to swing and punch away. Other wrestlers jumped into the melee; they had a hallway rumble.

Suddenly, there was a loud clap that frighteningly came from the opposite end of the darkened hallway. There, the ominous figure stood in the smoky shadows at the dimmed entrance to the lobby; it was Sir Sange! He had eyes fixed on Jenny, Officer Bowie, and Demarcus, as they tried to stop him once. He was expressionless, scarier than knowing what he had in his cold, cold heart and wicked mind.

"I knew something lurked down there in the dark!" Lumberjack Jones held his wooden stake in his hand. "I knew it! He would've killed us all down there."

"Tonight, there is going to be a great marriage ceremony with a toast of your blood," stated Sir Sange. "I will be back for you all after nightfall!"

"It's still daylight!" Lumberjack Jones shouted, "Let's get him while he's weak!"

Sange angrily pushed a button on the nearest wall! The same kind of protective fire door on the other side of the hallway quickly slammed shut on the frightened crowd that suddenly conjured the will to live and attempted to rush him with wooden stakes. He then pulled the wires from the wall, which deactivated the opening and unlocking mechanism of the door and also cut the hallway lights. This time around, he schemed to use the presence of darkness at his tamed and contorted advantage, as a weapon to wipe out everybody.

The rescue remnants of the town and the weekend entertainers were hopelessly trapped and bound for a bloody onslaught at nightfall in the precinct hallway. They sat in the lightlessness, listened to distant gunshots and cries of their helpless townsmen, and watched the sun go down through the small opening of the side door with the hope that their little wooden stakes were sufficient for all vampires and their plan of attack was not foolhardy.

Chapter 8

Holy Smoke

Only the outlying brilliance of many dimmed dimples on our mystic moon illuminated and glowed upon the growing crowd of blood-thirsty vampires throughout the city of San De Juan. Inside the conquered police precinct, it was cigarettes and lighters that brought reassurance to the bleak situation that was faced by the imprisoned. Although the nightfall begat more and more hissing of prowling and thirstiest of creatures, the captured alliance prayed for forgiveness; the brightness of heavenly hope overshadowed their murky glimmer of determination.

"I am in love with your mother," stated Officer Bowie. He turned to Jenny. "I am done pretending with this! I am here in this hallway with you all because she means everything."

"I already know."

"You do?"

"My mother talks in her sleep about you all the time. I've even spied on her phone conversations with you. I know she's into you."

"So, do you approve?"

"I guess," replied Jenny. "She could do a lot worse. Who am I to judge? When we were at Skull Hill, I thought a vampire was best for her. Honestly, you're probably the best available man in our town for her. I know my glorious mother, a little vain, can be a handful."

"I can handle everything she throws my way."

Jessup interrupted, "Well… Not anymore. If Sange has Jenny's mother, forget about it. He's probably already bitten her and forked her a few times."

Demarcus shouted, "Shut up, Jessup! You know that you're always out of line."

"I'm out of line? Why don't you tell Jenny why you won't ask her out? Why don't you tell her why you're just stringing her along as if she was just some groupie when you know she's trying to show you time and time again that she wants to be more than friends?"

Jenny turned to Demarcus, as well as all of the professional wrestlers.

Demarcus replied, "I won't ask Jenny out because I put my boys first. Maybe that's a flaw? I'm a jock. Jessup, I know that you are interested in Jenny. I'm the star quarterback of the district and know that I'm an easy target for every female in the city. And from what I learned of my terrible father and loneliest mother is that the best wives start as best friends. I don't want to lose my boy or my best friend. I got time to date whoever, but for now, what's the rush when I am getting to know my best friends?"

Jessup nodded with approval. "So, Jenny, what's up? Do you want to go out with a hell of a guy? You know that people call me the Dump Truck in most circles. Jenny, will you be my girlfriend? Jenny, did you even hear my question?"

"I am in love with you," said Jenny to Demarcus. "Please, allow me to have at least one prayer answered. I will not beg you to ask me out, but I am totally into you."

"What?" Jessup smacked his lips. "You can't see me, Jenny? I'm right here!"

"Jessup is like a brother to me," said Jenny.

Jessup walked away towards the professional wrestling group to sulk and complain at the terrifying words any guy cannot take from a woman he wants. "I'm like a freaking brother?"

Accompanying Jessup's sorrow was the most popular professional wrestler named Big Momma Brown because of her 500-plus weight and her deaf-defying Butt Splash from the top rope onto her opponents. Many fans also saw her as sexy because she wrestled under a belly dancing character that wore sky blue leggings with a pair of thongs on top, a sports bra that supported her from knocking against her knees. She danced and gyrated her hips before and after each match. Jessup was all in! She dodged and moved past her fellow wrestlers, Crane and Lumberjack Jones, to give Jessup a big bear hug. If such was her last attempt at love, she was going out satisfied.

Jessup's other jock friends' mouths hung wide open, after all, she was famous!

"I think you're cute," she claimed to Jessup. "You're a senior in high school, but I graduated from high school last year. Maybe you and I can talk?"

Jessup's friends were in awe. The other professional wrestlers nodded in approval. The kid, Jessup, had possible pro wrestling potential with his size and heart. If football didn't work out after he graduated from high school, perhaps professional wrestling would be in his cards. He would have a pretty good headstart and girlfriend in the famous Big Momma Brown.

"Did you all hear that?" Jessup declared, "Big Momma Brown has a crush on me!"

"Do you want to talk, Dump Truck Jessup?"

Officer Bowie shouted, "Go get her, boy!"

Right as Jessup strutted by the hallway side door and reached for Big Momma Brown, a pale, ashy hand with black nails reached for his arm! The vampires outside the hall were ready to feast! Suddenly, the car that blocked that very same side door moved forward. The side door slowly opened!

Big Momma Brown grabbed Jessup out of the way, as the fearless vampires rushed into the crowded hallway! The high schoolers and pro wrestlers stabbed at the thirsty beasts, but there were so many creatures that entered. The defeat was palpable for many of those that fought for their life.

The undead got replenished; it was only a matter of time before Sir Sange would make an entrance to fulfill his promise to drink the blood from Officer Theodore Bowie, Jenny Achebe, and Demarcus Peller. He planned to share his drink in the coming hours of the night, as she stared upon his bride-to-be that slept in a nightmare of his dark magic. She would be of confusing thirst if he awakened her, so he planned to bite her when he had that promised, celebratory glass of blood in hand. Now, it was the time to make his presence known in that hallway to start the fulfillment of his familiar legacy.

"No!" shouted Sir Sange. He suddenly sensed massive deaths to his vampires in the hallway! He turned away from the bride-to-be. "No, this cannot be! I must stop this!"

Back in the hallway, the tables turned on the vampires. Officer Bowie and Demarcus protected Jenny, and with one last stab of their opponents, they watched vampires scream in agony and die throughout the hallway! Officer Bowie stepped towards the middle of the hall. He observed a dying vampire that burned to the ground right in front of him; it turned to ashes.

There was water suddenly sprinkling throughout the hallway, which landed upon everyone. Warm-blooded humans waved their arms to protect from drowning, while vampires cried in agony! The vampires could not surrender into any dry spaces, nor could they escape through the side door, as it was blocked by two individuals that wore tanks on their back with hoses that shot the liquid. Soon, vampires outside of the hallway retreated. Inside, the remaining vampires caught flame underwater and burned into ashes. Cheers arose from those who survived the vampires' onslaught.

Jessup hugged Big Momma Brown. They kissed and slobbered all over one another for the first time. Other professional wrestlers and high schoolers gave one another high fives. Jenny and Demarcus embraced.

"What just happened?" Officer Bowie looked past the crowd of victors.

A figure made his way towards the officer and stepped over the human ashes. It was none other than Detective Vincent Bradbury.

Officer Bowie asked, "How did you guys know that would work? What's in the tanks?"

"It is holy water, blessed. With faith, God has no master." His partner declared. "Our people from the local church are also at war with these evil things in this hour. Detective Prendergast and I noticed that during the onslaught, the retreating vampires or bats were flying here. Then we saw them engage this hallway. It looks like we got here just in time. Only five of you took the bite. Three of those individuals got staked."

Lumberjack Jones and Crane high-fived one another and looked down at the three they body-slammed, delivered a pile-driver to, and then stabbed with their wooden stakes.

"You said five got bit?" Officer Bowie asked. "Where are the other two?"

"They're right behind you," whispered Jessup.

Officer Bowie jumped away and towards Detective Prendergast. He ducked behind the detective and frowned upon the site of Jenny and Demarcus. During the hallway war, Demarcus had been bitten and then snuck a bite on Jenny. Now, they hissed and had long fangs.

"I take it back, Officer Bowie," said Jenny. "I don't want you to marry my mother. I want to take a bite out of you instead if that's okay with my boyfriend."

Demarcus hissed. "Of course, that is okay. I have not asked you out yet."

Jenny looked over the entire hallway with delight to drink from everyone, or at least for the Sir Sange to make a blood bath of everyone. After all, he now stood in the doorway with Detective Bradbury's dead sidekick in his arms.

Lumberjack Jones ran and tried to dropkick the master vampire. Sange's backhand met him upside the head. Jones flew towards the opposite end of the hallway with a broken neck. His constituents hovered around him to help him with first aid.

A high school football player bravely dove at the unimpressed vampire, but with humongous disregard, Sir Sange grabbed the kid in mid-air and tore him in half like cheapened one-ply toilet tissue.

"After I destroy the rest of these insignificant morons, Officer Bowie, I'm coming for you. I will share your blood with my bride!" Sange threatened. "And you, Detective Bradbury, are in the way with your stupid little toys! For what you have done to mines, I am going to get ahold of you and release the greatest of wrath on you."

Detective Bradbury walked over and stood alongside Officer Bowie. He whispered, "We have got to make this a more even fight. We cannot have these two behind us, while Sange is ahead of us. So, take the cross from my neck; I pray that you have some kind of faith in our creator."

Officer Bowie grabbed the crucifix from the detective's body and held it towards Jenny and Demarcus. He watched them cry and drop to the ground in surrender.

"No!" Sir Sange was not pleased for their pain, for it made for an unbearable pinch. Their cries were the screeching to his ears that painfully tore his eardrums. Of his bearing, they were an extension of his being, as well as all the vampires. "Stop that! I beg of you to put the cross away, or I will destroy you in a torturous tiding! I'll kill all of you!"

Everybody in the hall was exhausted from the battle before Sange showed up. They backed up and readied for his attack.

Jenny cried out, "You're killing us, Officer Bowie! I thought that you loved me as much as you loved my mother? You put that cross away; I promise that I will make it all right!"

"I can't do this,' said Officer Bowie. He started to drop his hand down. "I cannot kill my girlfriend's daughter! There has got to be another way!"

"There is another way," stated Detective Bradbury. "I can hold them off here, but you'll need to go over there and kill Sange! That's the only way to restore these kids. Take my tank of water and take him out before he attacks everybody over there!"

Officer Bowie exchanged the crucifix for the tank of holy water and placed it over his back. He looked at Sange and shouted, "Come get some of this, you bastard!"

"If you want your girlfriend, you will put that toy away and allow me to take you to her," said Sange. "If you try me with that liquid, maybe it will work, and your Michelle will certainly die forever in my nightmarish sleep and never awake from it. Or maybe the water doesn't work because your faith is weak, and then I'll simply tear you from limb to limb, Mr. Bowie. You have worked several Sunday shifts and therefore missed quite a bit of church for years. Are you sure that you want to risk your girlfriend's life with your pint of faith, in which only you know that if you died today, your judgment would send you below us?"

Sir Sange chuckled, suddenly went stone-faced, with his blood still, red eyes of a furious and fiery sword that could stab a petrified redwood dead. He ghostly approached as if he floated on thin air. He passed Officer Bowie and wanted him to follow, beyond the blocked door. The officer, in doubt of his faith, was not given any more time to contemplate.

After the master vampire stopped and briefly smelled familiar blood and glanced at the familiar facial structure with the detective, he raised his hand towards the closed, jammed door, and it suddenly opened for him to walk through and into the dark space.

Sange signaled only for Officer Bowie to follow. The vampire planned to marry and turn her into the undead tonight. He wanted to also fulfill his vengeful promise for the cop to be tortured by watching.

To celebrate the wedlock, the vampire planned to painfully dismantle Officer Bowie's body, while alive, with bare hands and serve each blood dripping limb as a cup of communion with the new bride.

As the detective held Jenny and Demarcus at bay in the corner, with the crucifix, he said to the police officer, "It would be wise not to follow as close. If you walk through that door, you'd better watch your back. From readings of my ancestors, he is very strategic. He has a dreadful plan for you. You have to be aware of everything. Last but not least, I hope that you believe in God."

"Just because I don't go to church anymore does not mean that I am not strong in my faith," declared the officer. "Only God can judge me."

After Officer Bowie cautiously passed through the doorway, the storm door solidly shut.

Others who did not attend to Lumberjack Jones gathered around the detective. The detective held the two vampires at bay, in the corner, surrendered.

"Sir, how do you know about beating these creatures or have the guts to take them on like this?" asked Jessup. "You look as if you know what you're doing."

Jenny suddenly added, as if she was practiced in a trance, "Yes, detective, tell us how you are knowledgeable and possess these dastardly items that bring harm to us? Who are you?"

"Let's just say that these tools and teachings have been in my family for decades and some for centuries," said the detective. "Without us, vampires would rapidly run hostile throughout the world for centuries. I happen to be a descendent of the Van Helsing family; we are vampire slayers."

That name! Van Helsing caused a stir in the distinctive design of any and every vampire's genetic being, as his name telepathically transmitted from Jenny and Demarcus. As Sir Sange hastily led Officer Bowie to his makeshift tomb, he stopped to control his sudden rage at the name of Van Helsing. It was the birthright name of all the slayers he was defeated by for centuries!

Suddenly, the vampire's fantasy to kill Officer Bowie halted; it was now the bloodline of Van Helsing that he promised to grind into shredded meat and twist his bloody dry for the maximum reward. Officer Bowie and getting married was now a consolation to his night.

Demarcus chuckled. He strained to look up at Detective Prendergast.

"What is so funny?" asked the detective. "Why are you laughing?"

"Sange knows who you are," answered Demarcus, as the crucifix broke him down. "He knows your name; he is angry!"

Jenny chuckled also. She now appeared to be weakened and sore. "After he makes a game of your friend, Officer Bowie, he is coming back to get you. He plans to destroy everyone helping you and anyone related to you, Van Helsing. This day will be the last stand of your family!"

Big Momma Brown, the giant professional wrestling phenomenon, worriedly said to her friends, "The police officer said that he hasn't gone to church in years! Where I come from, going to church is essential. I don't believe in that nonsense. That police officer is doomed! And by the way, those two young monsters are talking, so is that guy holding the crucifix!"

Others tried to argue her beliefs in the church, but she was Big Momma Brown. Her voice was as large as her size. "Once that guy with the crucifix gets juked with the necklace, those vampires will take him out! The way I see it is that the side door there is wide open. I can see that there are a few police cars out there, from here. Does anybody know how to hotwire cars? I say that we pick up Lumberjack Jones and get the hell out of this town! We have wooden stakes. All this stuff is their fight and not ours, over some girl. Let's go!"

The other wrestlers suddenly agreed. Some knew how to hotwire cars too.

"Wait!" Jessup stood in front of Big Momma Brown, as his weary classmates stood behind him. "I live in this town. We need to win, or my entire town dies! Please stay, Big Momma. All we have to do is defeat Sir Sange! Besides, I thought you and I were going to give it a try. I don't want you to leave me!"

"I'm sorry," said Big Momma Brown, "but we have a chance to fight out there than to sit here and count on that old detective guy or the police officer. Anyways, who trusts in police these days? I don't, not where I live. They shoot innocent, unarmed people where I live."

Crane, another wrestler, disagreed. "Not all police are dirty, Big Momma. However, you are right! That cop is just one guy. He wasn't a priest! Did you see that spook he went after? He was near seven feet tall and had fangs, man!"

The detective added, "He does not have to be a priest to kill a vampire. He has to have faith, not simply to follow the rules like a robot, but to have a genuine relationship with God!"

All of the wrestlers were ho-hum with the preaching. They took their wooden stakes, picked up an injured Lumberjack Jones, and loaded up in the police vehicles.

"Those wrestling goons are not going to get far in those cars," spat Demarcus. He covered his eyes with his shirt from the crucifix. "He's watching them too. The sky is covered with bats! As soon as he finishes with the police officers, he'll get them!"

Chapter 9

The Toast

As Officer Theodore Bowie cautiously walked through the demolished Administration department, he warily watched everything and aimed at anything that seemed to move. There was a still, cold air about, as his mind played mirage tricks of shadows throughout. His fears boiled over as he saw bloody corpses, slain over chairs for the vampire's thirst. There were familiar bodies laid on floors and over the counters.

The glass door to the sheriff's office slowly opened. A thick mist of smoke shielded all of the windows, so he could not see inside. The police officer pulled the wooden stake from his pocket and held the nozzle that ran from the tank on his back.

"Where is Michelle?" Officer Bowie demanded. "Where is my girlfriend?"

Sange's hand popped out of the midst nearly two feet from the officer's head. The vampire waved his hand, and the smoke moved away from the center of the office space. The midst formed a barrier so thick, you could not see through it, across the windows of the sheriff's office.

In the corner of the room, the thick smoke cleared away. Officer Bowie saw that his girlfriend was asleep in an elegant mahogany wood coffin, lined with soft, white velvet padding.

"You killed her?"

"She is asleep until I wake her," answered Sange. "At what price would you ask me to wake her, Officer Bowie? Would you say, give your life?"

"I did not come here to play games or negotiate. Give me back my girlfriend!"

"I'm afraid that I will not do such a thing," replied Sange.

"Then, I will negotiate my life for hers. I need to know that she is alive!"

"You're in no place to negotiate!" Sange approached Officer Achebe. He lowered his head to her neck. "I am going to enjoy all of this. You shall suffer from jealousy and envy. Then I will torture you with a slow and painful death after I quench my thirst for blood."

"Get away from her!"

Officer Bowie squeezed the trigger and water shot from the nozzle, but his nervousness subjected his aim to douse the casket! Sir Sange disappeared in the midst.

The worried officer looked around the room. A shadow glided throughout the smoke. Suddenly, Sange stood right beside him! The vampire ripped the holy water dispenser from Officer Bowie's back, and it fell into the foggy floor!

"Now I shall make quick death of you," stated the vampire. He quickly picked up the police officer by his neck, before he could gather the tank of holy water, and walked him to the coffin. "Take a good look, policeman. She is going to be my bride! Then, together we will feed off of you to celebrate our destiny of death forever."

"No! You bastard, don't you touch her! Get away from her! No! Get away from her, you son of a bitch!"

"The time has come."

Sir Sange easily held the policeman in one hand, and with the other, he lifted the back of his bride-to-be's head and passionately sunk his fangs so deep into her neck, all the officer saw was the vampire's gum and webs of her thinned blood.

The master of the undead bloodied the novice of the ceremony. Sir Sange's bloody eyes rose into his forehead!

His everlasting curse, of his being, seeped into her surrendered body. Her thinned blood was so unexpectedly sweet and desired for centuries that the vampire went into a moaning orgasm and frenzy! Then, his body went completely numb with satisfaction and glory.

The vampire was in a euphoric state and nearly forgot that he did not plan to kill her by sucking her dry. He forgot that he held the police officer by the neck and unconsciously let the officer go! Officer Achebe's blood was so tasty and addictive to the vampire that he guzzled more of her blood, while he also lost telepathic control of Jenny and Demarcus in the hallway and his hold on the storm doors.

Bats above the city lingered; the dark skies became confused when Sange became disconnected. Now, bats flew without order or instruction. Most vampires walked around the town like purposeless zombies or just stared into the air. His thirst for his newborn bride's blood was so satisfying that he dropped to his knees, dropped his head, and savored every drop of her blood between his fangs.

Officer Bowie saw that he had a chance to grab the container of holy water! He dove to the other end of the office, grabbed the tank and nozzle, and returned to where he last saw Sange.

"Where'd he go?" Officer Bowie aimed right and left, as he could not find the vampire! "Detective, did you see where he went?"

Suddenly, a drop of blood landed on the tip of the police officer's nose! Sir Sange sprawled out across the ceiling, above!

"Look out!" cried Detective Prendergast, who advanced further into the precinct and kicked in the sheriff's office door upon Sange's hungover euphoria. He noticed Sange on the ceiling and immediately pulled out his crucifix! He held up the holy symbol to Sange!

"No!" The vampire angrily retreated to the other side of the smoky office. The detective was indeed strong with his faith in God, as the vampire learned.

Jessup and his high school football friends showed up at the sheriff's office door. "We put Jenny and Demarcus in a cell. They tried to trick us and acted as if they were so confused about what happened. Then they showed their fangs! We beat the shit out of them and threw them into a cell. So, is everything here, okay? Did we defeat that pale ass demon? How are our friends?"

Sir Sange violently slammed the office door shut in the teenagers' faces with his unearthly powers from across the room and kept the spell on it to stay closed. He slowly levitated from the smoky corner of the office. He smirked, for his undead bride had awakened and sat up. She only looked at her master.

"Michelle?" Officer Bowie pointed the water nozzle at her and then Sange. She was very pale and was expressionless. He declined to be defeated. "Michelle!"

"Michelle belongs to me now!" Sir Sange conquered his passion. "Drinking her blood, I have never felt more alive! Officer Bowie, it pleasures me to say to you that it felt like making love to your old lady, but now Michelle and I share an intimacy that goes beyond your dwarfed twig and authoritative ego. Through my authority, I pronounce her as my bride!"

"Man, I'll kill you!" The officer declared. "I'll swear it!"

Detective Bradbury warned the officer. "He's baiting you! Do not let him throw you off your faith or game! You know what you believe, and you must focus, officer!"

Sange smiled. "If the detective can finish with facetious comments, we can all move on. Both of you will serve up as a bloody toast to Michelle and our everlasting marriage. Officer, I'll let her choose which limb to tear off of you and drink from, but you, Detective Prendergast, I heard you say that you're a filthy descendent of Van Helsing. That changes everything."

Many decades of bitter and tortured endings suddenly crossed the vampire's mind; his eyes grew red with those memories: Fiery deaths by sunlight, death by beheadings, and so on.

"I should have recognized the stench of your blood from the start!" Then the angry vampire vehemently stated, "I am going to rip your head from your body, claim the victory over your namesake, and drink your entire head dry of every ounce of your blood! Allow my bride to join me now, as we make a toast."

The bride hissed and suddenly climbed from the casket and stood next to Sange. She wore a plain white, colonial-type gown, obviously from a museum or second-hand store that the vampire patronized after he kidnapped her. Her face was pale; her reddened eyes shrunk. She opened her mouth and showed fangs for a second!

"Theodore, are you afraid of me? Why? You know that I would never hurt you. I am okay; I was just sleeping. Hug me, Theodore. Come here." She took a few more small steps towards Officer Bowie and held her hands out for a hug.

"Michelle, please stay the hell away from me." Officer Bowie reluctantly stood his ground and readied his hand on the nozzle with his finger on the trigger, as she slowly approached him.

Detective Prendergast was not confident any longer in his ability to stop the authoritative beast. He had only read the many tales of vampire defeats in old books that got passed down through his family's generation as wise or folklore; there was nothing he could compare to this deathful quandary. To hell with the drama, he thought and tried to open the office door to escape. Sange's spell settled for the door to remain shut during the rest of the ceremony.

"You are a coward, Van Helsing off-spring, and with no testicular fortitude," said Sir Sange. He smelled the detective's fear. With his mind, he effortlessly lifted the overweight detective off the ground! "You piece of garbage, this is the luckiest night of my time on earth! You will pay for the many deaths of many vampires. I will drink from your body with fury, for the sake of all of us, I swear it!"

"Please kill him, Officer Bowie!" cried the detective. He kicked his legs and swam in suspended air. He could not escape Sir Sange's magic.

Officer Bowie watched the newly sinister smile of Sange's bride. She was about to bite the hell out of his neck, but he chose not to hurt her. So, he turned to Sange and sprayed the unexpected vampire king with the blessed, holy water from the tank on his back!

Sange furiously hissed and turned his attention from the detective to Officer Bowie.

His bride howled in burning pain, as her flesh was in sync with the horrifying demon; she retreated behind her master's casket!

With his silky cape burned and smoky from that holy water, the hostile Sir Sange became thoroughly full of increased rage with Officer Bowie. The vampire's face blistered with spots of holy water! He could not focus his magic on the plump detective anymore, so he waved his arms; the detective dropped to the floor like an asteroid!

"Ah, shit!" The detective had crashed into the floor so hard that his fibula snapped and protruded through his foot. He rolled in agony and waved his hands to clear the smokiness to see how he could help the detective. He thought for sure the master vampire would attack him, as his blood seeped from his pants leg!

Sange continued to use his cape, which protected his face. He had thought about the situation long enough.

Officer Bowie shouted, "Now let that be a lesson to you!"

Sir Sange speedily glided to the brave officer, ripped that water tank of holy water from his back, and kicked it out of reach. The vampire wrapped his hand completely around the officer's neck and shoved him down to the floor.

"You have the right to remain silent," whispered the damned. Sir Sange hissed and added, "Isn't this how you police officers do it? Yes, I believe it is so; I am going to destroy you, you moron!"

The bride asked, "Can I have the detective, while you attend to that police officer?" She smelled his blood that drizzled from his busted foot and was thirsty!

"No!" Sange shouted. "Van Helsing belongs to me, dear. Now, I want you to stand there and watch me destroy this little man for you. I want your first drink to come from him!"

As soon as Sange opened his mouth to bite and suck the blood from Officer Bowie, perhaps beheading him out of rage, the vampire suddenly felt a wooden stake hit him upside his dome!

"Damn," stated the failed detective. He threw his well-crafted ebony stake at the unaware vampire and prayed that it would pierce, but it was the back end of the stake that bounced off of Sir Sange's noggin.

Officer Bowie cried out, "Oh, God, help me! What have I done? Please, God!"

"Help you?" Sange laughed, along with his bride in sync. "Police officer, you have no authentic faith in your Master, hiding behind a church symbol such as holy water as described in some bible context of Numbers 5:17. I will tell you what you are. You are a hypocrite and a heathen to the kingdom of God! You have gone to church before, but you don't live the life of a believer. Aren't you supposed to read the holy book for instruction and guidance and pray to your Creator for life? Yet, you call on your Creator only when you're in trouble. Help me! I need help. Woe is me. I pity you!"

The officer continued to cry his heart out! However, a sudden thought crossed his mind. He still had a stake in his pants pocket. The wooden stake thrown by the detective was next to his other pocket.

"You are just like all of the rest of the humans in the world today," scorned the malicious vampire. "This world today is much too easy for me to rule! There are too many humans wanting some higher being to do things their selfish way instead of through divine truth. You and that scoundrel over there are nothing more but the foulest dirt of the ground. I shall thirst no more!"

The detective briefly smiled back at Sir Sange. He declared, "You cannot judge humanity. You're simply a murderer!"

"Yes, I can! I have the power of eternity and the power of death in my possession. In other words, that makes me a god and not a murderer! So, I say now, enough with the small talk and on with my judgment. You both are guilty, and it's time to quench the thirst of your blood for all vampires throughout time!"

The detective yelled to the crying cop, "Believe, Officer Bowie! Believe in God, and do not listen to the vampire's lies about you! Your faith is your walk with the Lord and not his! Take hold of life in your hands and think about the wooden cross!"

The raged vampire took his eyes off of the police officer to scowl at the detective. That was the start of Sange's demise. With the officer's faith in God and the detective's wooden hint, the vampire deemed helpless and withered to the sight of two wooden stakes held together to form a crucifix held by Officer Bowie. Officer Bowie stood to his feet, as tears streamed from his face!

The officer was a repetitive and regular sinner that always believed in God! By no means was the officer a perfect man, but who was that vampire or any man on the earth to say or judge anyone else's journey? At some point, if not too late, men can be redeemed.

"I'm not a believer?" The officer screamed at Sange. He then quoted childhood scriptures of the Bible like John 3:16 and Psalms 23, for he was not a recent bible reader, and he stuttered throughout prayer for complete forgiveness. "Who are you tell me what my walk is with God? I'm no priest, like the ones in the movies, but the Lord has always been my father. He is my friend! So, you can go to hell!"

"Put that cross away!" screamed the vampire. "I'll let you go! I'm sorry, Theodore! I'm so sorry! I'll give you back the girlfriend!"

The police officer did not look at the bride. She dropped to the floor and screamed her head off for him to stop praying to God. She begged him to drop the stakes! She reminded him that he hadn't been to church in years. She said everything to put him down. She even mentioned that his divorce was his fault. She tried to disrupt him. Yet, Officer Bowie overcame a hissing Sange, who retreated into his casket. He was too weak to close the casket door himself!

"Do it now!" yelled the detective.

Officer Bowie looked at the surrendered vampire one last time. Boldly, he pounded a stake into the heart of Sange! Then the officer took the other stake and used it for a hammer. He angrily beat the wooden stake through Sange's heart to the casket sheets; the vampire could not free himself!

Suddenly, screams of terror howled throughout the town! The bats in the sky fell to the ground and turned back into men and women of the counties.

"Ah shit," mumbled Paul Glasgow. He was one of the bats that fell from the sky, but he landed on an automobile and exploded in a paintball stain on the hood. He burped alcohol fumes and died.

The survived pro wrestlers, on the road, watched the clouds go away and celebrated the apparent victory.

Meanwhile, the cop's partner, Officer Michelle Achebe, fell asleep in the corner of the sheriff's office.

"Did we get him?" Jessup and his jock pals suddenly kicked in the sheriff's door, which no longer was shut under Sange's magic. "Is he dead?"

Everybody looked down over the magnificent casket and watched the withering vampire's skin fold, curdle down to his organs, and materialize to his skeletal bones. Soon after, the vampire's bones fell to ashes. He was defeated as the relieved officer dropped one of his stakes and kneeled next to his former partner. Was she still a vampire? The officer readied his one stake, as the high schoolers watched her awaken.

"Michelle?"

Slowly, his partner awoke and opened her eyes. She spoke without fangs. "Theodore?"

"Michelle!" The officers hugged one another.

"Oh, Theodore, what happened? You saved me; I love you!"

"Can somebody get us out of this jail cell?" called a familiar voice from a distance. It was Demarcus Peeler. "Hello, is anyone in the police station?"

"Let us out!" hollered Jenny.

Led by Jessup, the football jocks dashed out of the sheriff's office and assisted their friends they locked up earlier. They shared how awful Demarcus and Jenny were as vampires, but the lovers had no recollection. Nor did the two lovers understand how they got black eyes, swollen lips, knots all over their forehead, and various sprains throughout their bones.

Jessup whistled a tune and placed his bloodied hands in his pocket, as did the other jocks that followed his lead. Nobody ever mentioned how they beat the hell out of those two; it was in self-defense, mostly.

Theodore, Michelle, and Jenny blissfully embraced. It was indeed a new day.

Detective Prendergast finally got helped to his feet and led to the marvelous coffin. He warily celebrated along with Officer Bowie and Achebe in the success of Sange's defeat for the time being. However, he knew deep down inside that the cursed prisoner of between worlds would thirst to walk the earth again. After all, there were other urns with Sange's ashes in as many countries as there strategically were descendants of Van Helsing nearby.

The detective bloody hoped and prayed that Sir Sange would never again resurrect in his lifetime. Exhaustedly, he left the precinct to return home, buried the ashes in a disclosed location, and inked his experience of Sir Sange in the continued Van Helsing diary. He entitled the chapter: The Thirst for Blood.

978-0-9796219-7-0